CONTEMPORARY AMERICAN FICTION

THE QUIET ENEMY

Author of two novels, *Charleyhorse* and *The Live Goat*, winner of the Harper Saxton Prize, Cecil Dawkins was born in Alabama and grew up there. She received her B.A. from the University of Alabama and her M.A. from Stanford. She also received a Stanford Writing Fellowship, a Guggenheim Fellowship, and an NEA grant. Her play, *The Displaced Person*, based on stories by Flannery O'Connor, was produced off-Broadway. Her ⌐ories have appeared in *Paris Review*, *Southwest Review*, ⌐*anee Review*, and other magazines. Cecil Dawkins ⌐ New Mexico.

THE
QUIET ENEMY

CECIL DAWKINS

PENGUIN BOOKS

PENGUIN BOOKS
Viking Penguin Inc., 40 West 23rd Street,
New York, New York 10010, U.S.A.
Penguin Books Ltd, Harmondsworth, Middlesex, England
Penguin Books Australia Ltd, Ringwood, Victoria, Australia
Penguin Books Canada Limited, 2801 John Street,
Markham, Ontario, Canada L3R 1B4
Penguin Books (N.Z.) Ltd, 182–190 Wairau Road,
Auckland 10, New Zealand

First published in the United States of America by Atheneum 1963
Published in Penguin Books 1986

LIBRARY OF CONGRESS CATALOGING IN PUBLICATION DATA
Dawkins, Cecil, 1927–
The quiet enemy.
(Contemporary American fiction)
I. Title.   II. Series.
PS3554.A943Q5   1986   813'.54   86-8174
ISBN 0 14 00.8011 2

Printed in the United States of America by
R. R. Donnelley & Sons Company, Harrisonburg, Virginia
Set in Bembo

TO MY MOTHER

AND

TO THE MEMORY OF MY FATHER

THE QUIET ENEMY

EMINENT DOMAIN

SHE sat slowly rocking on her sloping porch, its boards white from much scrubbing with lye and scalding water. She sat behind morning-glory vines that climbed trellises of string to the roof. The blossoms had closed. From out on the road the vines looked dense, but she could see through them with her keen eyes. Her old fingers felt numb when she touched surfaces of things, and she had no sense of the thing she touched. In her ears she might have carried pebbles of chalk for all the sound she got through them. But her eyes could pinpoint a lark in flight though it be but a speck against the yellow sky. And seeing, she could imagine its song. No longer her ears, but her eyes gave sounds to her.

Now from the length of the shadows, from the translucent green of the tender leaves, she knew the afternoon time of the locust was past, the time of the locusts' plaintive why-oh-why-oh-why. Now the crickets would be snipping answers—because-because. Her eyes gave sounds to her—old sounds remembered from time before the pebbles lodged in her ears. But she could not heed the sounds now, because of that web of troubling that had spun itself out in her. So, in silence, she rocked.

The trouble had been growing in her for a long time. The winter just past had been a hard one and the wind had howled through her house. And then in April, when the buds swelled, a late frost came, aborting the spring. Now it was summer, a dry one, the driest in a long spell of drought years. She no longer felt heat, now she was so old, but she felt the dryness in her brown skin shrunk tight on her skull, slick as scar skin. And now, like wind or water, dust seeped under doors and through chinks in her house and she must sweep each day if the place was to show she lived there still.

Across the road lay the barren field. Sowing time was past, and the days of harvest had come. But the field had known no planting and only the dry stalks of last year's cotton, which should long since have been plowed under, leaned picked bones to earth. The troubling grew each time she looked at the field. As the sun was her clock, marking the hours, that field was her calendar and had for many years told the seasons. Now the page of the calendar went unturned and the sun clock circled like a free-spinning cog that turns no wheel.

And there had been other signs. She had gone early one morning, scavenging along the woods for broom straw, aimlessly moseying toward Tillett's barn.

When she came there, she saw at once that barn and pasture were empty. Strangers with claw-tooth hammers clamored over the house. Already the roof was gone. Plunderers, she thought. Hidden in the blackberry switches, she watched the house of Tillett, where she'd worked out her working years, being torn to the ground. She forgot her broom straw, and after that for many days her house went unswept.

Then the white man came to her. He was thick and damp and he spread his hands before her and moved his lips and wiped his face. At last, worn out from walking up and down her narrow porch, he took out the paper and pointed his finger over the lines, his mouth shaping words. Then he unclipped his pen from his pocket, and with his hand shoving hers, traced her mark on the paper. After that he turned jovial, slapped his thigh, put on his hat, and waved her good day. She undid the tobacco plug she kept knotted in the end of her shawl and bit off enough of it to comfort her tongue while she watched his automobile creep and twist with the road till it was out of sight and she was shut of him.

But she was not easy. For of late many people had moved along the road. In wagons piled high with bureaus and bedding and straight-backed, cane-bottomed chairs they moved. And plunderers were upon the Tillett place where she'd worked out her working years. And there was the field, the barren field, left for a harvest of dry, deceiving maypops after the passion flowers grew.

As she sat and puzzled and rocked, she looked westward down the road. A figure came swinging along. He wore no hat and his skin was fine black and glistening. Even at a distance she saw the glistening on his face and saw his puckered lips.

Jethro was whistling. He had money in his pocket. Not only the jingling coins, but wadded money as well. A week's pay. And he was free for the night and the morning. He'd heard of a town at the end of this long red road. There he was headed with money in his pocket and a night and a morning for spending and revel. He nursed the thirst he meant to quench, and his whistle was strident and shrill as he swung down the road, feeling the sand shifting under his canvas shoes and the savored strength and fullness in his thighs that he meant, too, to quench, to spend, in the town. His overalls were loose on him, hanging from galluses on his shoulders barely to touch his body. He wore no shirt, for Jethro disliked clothing in the summertime and wore only the overalls, which he didn't much mind for they were loose and touched his body furtively and whispered between his legs as he swung along, whistling his braggadocio tune.

As he approached, he eyed the house. It was no white man's house he knew from the slant of the porch, the lean of the chimney, and yet, withal, the morning-glory vines and the smell of lye.

Jethro paused on the road. He looked for the sun and saw only its lingering light. He squinted down the

6

road. No town in sight yet. He had a way to go. A drink of cool water would be good. Not much of a drink, but enough to wet his whistle. He was in no hurry. Jethro never was. Hurry was what caught a man, laid him in chains. He'd learned to take his time. He swung into the yard and saw her there, behind the vines.

'Hi-oh,' he gave her. 'Hi-oh, Old Mother. Got a dipper of water for a dried-out Jethro?'

He rested a foot on her step. 'Whoo-ee! Jethro one hot baby, Old Momma.'

He studied her taut-skinned old face, her gnome hands clutching the edges of her brown shawl.

'Old lady don't care for Jethro's comp'ny.' He laughed. 'Old lady don't like Jethro. You smaht, Old Lady.' He laughed. 'Just you keep set whilst I hunts up the water and be's on my way.' He stepped onto the porch and stretched until his fingers touched the roof.

She'd stopped rocking and stared straight ahead of her onto the darkening road. He walked behind her chair, laughing, and swooped to hang his face upside-down before her eyes. She started. He threw back his head, laughing. 'Cat got your tongue, Old Momma?' He peered through the screen door. 'Anybody here with you, Old Lady?' He pulled open the screen and poked his head inside. 'Whereabouts you hide your well?' He turned. She was standing close behind him. He grinned. 'You slick, ain't you,' he said. 'I ain't heard you move.'

He went whistling through the parlor and into the lean-to kitchen, where he saw steam rising from pots on the stove. He touched a lid, yanked back his smarting fingers, and licked them, laughing. 'Smell good,' he said. Then he saw the well shed in the yard. 'There he.' He slammed out the back door.

He dropped the bucket over the lip of the well and cupped his ear in his hand to hear the splash. 'Splut!' he said. He drew up the bucket and took the dipper gourd off its nail. The water was sweet and cold. He swished it around in his mouth. His eyes moved to the garden. The tomato bushes were staked and mulched with straw. The spindly corn was tasseled out, the ears beginning to swell.

'How much land you got here, Old Momma?' he asked. 'Nuff for you to get rich off it?' He looked back at her where she stood in the door. 'How come you still lives here? How much they give you for all this?' Her eyes narrow and filmed with secrets, her hands stealing under her sleeves to hide, she watched.

Jethro began to whistle again, this time a thin high whistle through his teeth. He rehung the dipper on its nail and walked to the door. Her hand stole toward the wire latch, but his arm shot out and, laughing, he yanked the door open.

Inside the kitchen he leaned against the door frame, close to her. She edged away and went to fiddle at the stove.

'Smell real good,' Jethro said. 'Aim to eat a little

8

supper now, Old Momma?' She did not look at him. She stirred the pot.

Jethro picked a straw from the broom and chewed on its end. He felt the weight of his money against his leg. He thought of the town. Then, 'Hit's early yet, Old Momma.' He laughed. 'I believe Jethro just take his supper here with you.' Having decided, he set about making himself useful. Plates came off shelves, chairs up to the table. 'You sho the talkin'est woman Jethro ever seen,' he said. He took the wooden spoon from her hand and stirred the pot. 'Um-umh! Turnip greens and all that pot likker and white meat. Umh! That cawn bread Jethro smell?'

As she moved between table and stove, the old woman gave no sign she remembered he was there. They sat and ate together. She kept her eyes down. She was used to eating alone, and she felt a sense of outrage to be watched at food. But now and then her sharp eyes flicked at him.

When they were through, dark had come. Jethro trimmed the wick with his switchblade knife and lit the lamp. 'There he. Now lemme see what all you got here.' Her eyes followed him as he took the lamp through the rooms, the parlor with its stiff chair and table and cot and the room where she slept in the white iron bedstead. 'All this yourn? All this here belong to you, Old Woman?'

He turned his eyes upon her and studied her. 'You cain' talk, can you, Old Woman?' And then, 'And you cain' heah no word I say.'

9

He threw back his head and laughed, his mouth so wide the old woman could see his pink gums and his white, flashing teeth and his two gold fills. She edged toward the door and stood there, showing she meant him to go. He pushed the door open and thrust her out onto the porch and into her rocker. He sat on the top step and stretched his legs into the yard. He began to whistle, no more the strident, shrill song he carried in his head when he carried money in his pocket, no more the thin, high whistle through his teeth, but now a tuneless, breathy whisper of a whistle came from him as a cloak to cover thought. Jethro's brain was turning over all this he had found beside the road.

'Here you got all this, Old Momma,' he said, looking at her set profile, cleft at her sunken mouth. 'And Jethro got nothing but work and worry. And I bet you don't know about that dam Jethro building up the valley there a ways. And I bet you don't know come not too long this here house lay down and die in a watery grave forty–fifty feet deep.' He studied her. She sat silent and perfectly still, like a thing in hiding. He laughed into the crickety night, flung out an arm and shoved her chair to rocking. 'Rock on, Old Momma,' he said. Her hands clutched the arms of the chair, but she did not look at him.

From the bib of his overalls he pulled tobacco and paper. He tapped out the coarse-ground leaf, rolled it, and with a flick of his tongue licked it sealed. When he struck the match, her eyes jumped over him. He had waited for that. 'Caughtcha!' he said.

'Well now, Old Momma—' he stood up—'Jethro just be on his way.' He stepped into the yard. 'But Jethro don't forget you, Old Momma. Jethro got lots of questions he aim to answer in that town.' And, before he set out, he reached and set the chair to rocking again.

She waited until she felt that she was alone. Then she went into her house, dragging her rocker in after her, and lowered the big wooden beams in place across her doors. She blew out the lamp and, in the dark now, and alone, knew she'd had the devil come to sup with her.

For a long time she sat in darkness. Now she knew the name of the troubling. The devil had taken this place for home, and the land grew nothing, and plunderers were at Tillett's, and the devil had driven the people out. All but her. And now he'd come. Finally, she knew what she must do. She lighted the lamp, but she kept the wick low. Then into the kitchen she went, and from the back of the pantry she drew powders and leaves and dried insect parts. These she measured and brewed until a strong smell, like old tea and forgotten spices, thickened the air in her house. Before dawn she slipped outside and in the darkness, her bold eyes growing accustomed, made her way to the stagnant pond at the foot of the garden. A cold-blood she must have. A leech was the thing, and next to that a young snake still in its first skin. But the old woman had to content herself with a frog. Then she trudged her way back to her heady kitchen and plunked the straining swelling frog into her brew. Onto it she clapped a lid and for a moment held it tight.

By morning she had the frog's bones ground to dust and strung in a cloth ball from a cord around her neck. If this wasn't enough, she had the devil she'd fashioned in the night, the cleft-foot devil with trident in hand, black as she'd seen him, standing in a circle of smelly leaves with a wick in his head. The old woman knew how to handle the devil. And in the morning she gathered the ripe things from her garden and did the work of the day as it must be done.

Her chores behind her, she sat, as it was her custom to sit, on her porch behind her concealing vines. For a time she amused herself by looking up the road, guessing what first she might see rounding the bend. But, as often happened these days, her watch waned as the road, yellow in the sunlight, remained empty but for the occasional traffic of a rabbit or a turtle. For three quarters of an hour she occupied herself with watching a black thing in the road a piece away. If it moved, showing itself to be a snake, that would be a sign she must interpret. But it did not move, and gradually she accepted it as a branch come to rest there. She set her chair to rocking, and there was the field before her, and the empty road. So she closed her eyes to the world in which only the shadows moved, and they imperceptibly.

As she dozed she was again aware, in the bright dry day, in the drought, of the pulling in her bones. In her young days as water witch, the pull would have prophesied rain and plenty. Now in these drought years of her life she could not spell its meaning. But the old woman knew a secret, a secret so fearful she'd kept it to herself. The old woman knew the land as an island under which the dark waters flow, silent and eternal. Sometimes they rocked her in her sleep. She knew the meaning of Moses' rod. For could she not, with her peach wand, find too the mystery that was always there for those who dared?

She dozed, feeling the pull of the waters strong in her bones, troubling about the meaning. She dozed into the late afternoon, and at sundown she dreamed of the snake in the road. Startled, she awoke, and her eyes sought the black limb in the ruts of the road. It was not there. She felt betrayed by her age that would let the wily snake beguile her. Then she gripped her chair. The black thing skinned out over her head to dandle itself before her, clinging to nothing.

She hunched low, lower, as it hovered, moved, dropped. Then she saw the fingers holding the stick. She wrenched herself around.

Jethro leaned against her door, smiling. 'Old Momma,' he said, 'you a sly old thing. But Jethro done caught you napping.' She clutched the arms of the rocker, steadying it. She made her breathing shallow, drawing her life in like a candlewick close to its fuel. She could not move her eyes from the stick he swatted around in the air. His balance there was unsteady. In his other hand hung a whisky bottle, half full. 'Hot,' he said and, to make her understand, he lolled out his tongue and panted like a feist. He lifted his face and turned up the bottle. She watched his throat pulse.

'Jethro celebrating, Old Momma,' he said. 'Bes' you be celebrating too.' He lurched forward, catching himself on her chair, and, yanking her head back by the cotton bolls of hair, while her old eyes started and her throat convulsed, he poured whisky at her sunken mouth, giggling his high, thin giggle.

Coughing, she knocked the bottle away and tried to wipe the whisky from her front.

'That the first sound I heard you make.' He knelt in front of her, hanging his head close to her stiffened face. And he said, 'Meet your newborn son Jethro, Old Momma.'

Her hands darted to his chest and she pushed, thrusting forward the rocker to send him toppling backwards down the steps and into the yard. For a moment he lay still. Then, raising his wet face, he shook himself. Edging toward her door, the old woman kept her eyes on him.

'You a mean old momma,' he said. 'Jest right for Jethro.' He picked up the fallen bottle, shook it, flung it away. He traced his fingers through the wet sand and put them to his tongue. Shuddering, he spat. From his hip pocket he pulled out a second pint, brushed it off, and still watching her, unplugged it with his teeth.

Poised, she waited for him to move his eyes from her and drink. And for a time he teased, holding the bottle half raised. Then, suddenly, he sprang, catching her while she waited there, and thrust her indoors and onto the daybed. 'There, Old Momma, you sit.'

He ranged through the house, picking up a slab of corn bread from the stove and cramming his mouth full. He found the furl of toasted bacon rind in her oven and brought it, with the remaining corn bread in its blackened pan, into the parlor and stood eating before her.

'I tell you something, Old Momma,' he said. 'Ifin they's a thing you wants to know, show 'em you ignorant, and they show you how smaht they be. Then pretty soon you as smaht as they is. And when they ast you questions, do like this,' and he put on innocence, casting his eyes to the ceiling and mincing in a circle. 'Shrug like this,' and he drew up his shoulders and spread his hands. 'Let they questions be they answers. You the old woman's boy? they ast. And Jethro shrug and put 'em off and in ripe time them niggers leading him over to that white man's land office.' He put out his hand and let himself be led by an invisible guide across the room. 'And they say, this here Jethro, Old Momma's onliest boy. White man, he ast, you know this boy, Jimero? They ain' gone show they ignorance. Jimero, old fool, say, I recollect oncet it was said she had a boy. And white man he say, Hazel, you know this nigger? And Hazel she think she roll oncet with Jethro and get herself a money bag, she say yes suh, this here Jethro, old woman's long-loss boy. And white man he say yeah, long-loss boys always turns up when Momma's got money up her stocking. And he say, shame on you, Jethro, leaving you mammy by herself all these years. And Jethro hung his head. Man say, you get her out of there. Get her some place to live outside the flood land. Do some good before you dies.' Jethro gulped his laughter. 'And that's when Jethro he promise to be a good boy to you, Old Momma.' He swung around to face her, his laughter rolling in tears down his face. 'And then they tole me how much money they put away for you up there at the bank. We rich, Old Momma!'

He washed more corn bread down with liquor and wiped his mouth. The old woman had drawn herself up small on the edge of the daybed. Her eyes did not leave his face. He had the powers, she knew, appearing out of nowhere, turning the snake to a willow wand in his hand. And she was old to meet the devil face to face. But now she knew it was to be.

She pulled herself up tall and went about her evening chores to show herself unafraid. Supper on, she went out into the dark in search of her goose. She stalked it through the brush at the edge of the woods, connived it into a fence corner, and caught it up. Jethro was at the door, waiting. He reached out to stroke the goose, but she covered it quickly with her shawl. Then, sitting in her rocking chair she began to pluck goose down into her apron.

Jethro leaned against the wall, sipping now and then from his bottle while he watched. 'Old Momma,' he said, 'Jethro gone to New Awleens. Jethro gone to where old sun smile on him ever last day in the year. Gone have heself a woman. What kind of woman? Black as a cave, wahm as a feather bed. No snow on her can she have. Black she be. And she wear no shoes on her feets, that one. Blossoms in her ears, have she. Red flowers without no thorns. And all night long when the sun done sunk, she cradle and rock rich boy Jethro, the livelong night, wahm rain outside on the roof.'

The old woman plucked the goose, her fingers fleet. Unsure now of his balance, the whisky hot in him, Jethro rolled his shoulders against the wall to some rhythm he found in his voice. His eyes now were not focused, and the whisky bottle hung by his side in the crook of his finger. 'Gone to New Awleens,' he sang. 'Gone to New Awleens. Yellow silk shirt with flowers on front and a walkin' stick and a house on stilts and a woman. Fat cigars and a fingah ring and a gold watch chain and a slick straw hat and a woman . . .'

The old woman's fingers plucked fast as she watched out from under her brows while his knees sagged and his eyes closed. The fire in the cook stove needed more wood, she knew, but she stayed where she was, plucking the goose.

Suddenly Jethro flung his empty bottle and rose up, laughing. It bounced off the screen and skidded across the floor to lie at her feet. He turned and pressed the length of his body to the wall. The old woman clutched the cowering goose.

Jethro peered at her from under his arm. He stumbled to her chair and hung over her, his shadow a hulk filling the room. His lips were gray and sweat stood in beads on his forehead. He reached, snatched the shawl from her shoulders, drew it about his own and sashayed in a circle. Then he came to her, looked down at the goose, grabbed it up, and closing one big hand over its head, gathered his muscles. The old woman saw the sudden blood, the feathers floating. The headless goose flopped about the kitchen, against the walls, spouting blood from its stump of neck.

Jethro fell on his knees, his face in her lap, shaking with laughter.

The old woman sat, not daring to move, for there he was—the devil, on his knees before her.

When the sun came through her window and fell on her face, she woke up. The devil was not there. The kitchen, which had been spattered to the ceiling with blood, was scrubbed and clean. On the sideboard, in her roaster, the headless goose lay, plucked and drawn and ready for the oven. Her body was cramped and tired from the night in the chair, but she was warm. Her shawl was wrapped around her shoulders, and the goose down warmed her lap.

She wondered if her mind had gone soft. Mulling it over, she built a fire in her stove and set the goose to cooking. She wished for a visitor, someone to come and sit by her, one she had known. She thought of the days when Tillett had stopped in. She felt it would be a good thing if she went walking while the dew was silver beads, before the sun claimed it and the wind raised the dust. A walk on the road would help her sort it all out, and she might meet a body there, walking. And passing, they might bow and nod.

First she went out to her well and drew a bucket of water. Then she washed herself, not waiting to heat the water but testing herself with its cold. She changed her clothing from the skin out and put on the apron that had lain in paper since the Tillett girl gave it to her one Christmas time. She took off her old slops and put on her black shoes with leather soles.

Well, she was an old woman, she told herself, and old women dream strange dreams. And the goose was old. She'd enough down for her pillow, and she was wise to eat the meat. She would die soon, and who then would have cared for the creature? She thought about dying. Here she was, dreaming of the devil. She chuckled to herself. Old women turn childish. She belonged to the Lord. He'd put His hand upon her when she was young and set her to His work of birthing and leading His children to the waters of life. How else could she have dared the devil so often with brews and incantations? No devil was going to get her now. She pictured death with its gate and, beyond, its people, all the faces she knew, waiting for her, leading her to a shade tree where she might rest and refresh and shed her age before she was led up to the house to meet the Lord.

By the time she'd dressed herself, the goose was spitting and the smell of roasting filled her house. She almost put off the walk, but she'd looked forward to it. And walking, she could look forward to returning to the goose. So, leaving her shawl behind, she set out. She tweaked a morning-glory from her vine and snuffed it. She put it in her mouth and felt the velvet of it on her tongue. The sun was warm. She saw a rabbit in the field, sitting in a furrow with his ears up. She paused at her step to look up the road. And there, in the distance, an old open truck crept toward her like a crippled bug. The driver, she could see, wore a blue shirt. She was so glad at the thought of meeting folk that she set out down the road toward them. He might stop in the road, and if she watched his lips she might understand him to say, 'Morning. Fine weather we having. Rain gone do a world of good.' And together they would study the guileless sky. And she longed to answer and to hear his voice. Would it be a stranger? Most like it would. She would speak if she could, and watch his lips move and try to answer. And maybe she would have him in to eat a bite. She strained her eyes, looking to see if behind him in the flat truck bed a woman sat. But she saw only the blue-shirted man as the strange thing neared, a fat coon tail jouncing on the radiator.

Jethro yanked the hand brake and slid to a halt beside her. Her mouth went dry. Was there no one left in all these hills and pockets but the devil and her? And now he came, decked out like a bridegroom in a new shirt, riding high in a steaming machine.

'Old Momma, you looking mighty pert. What all this you got on?' he shouted over the motor's din. 'All this for Jethro's coming?' He bent and held out his hand to her. She stood where she was. He leaped down and set her on the open seat and sprang back up again beside her. As the thing shuddered and started up, he dropped his arm across her shoulders. 'Old Momma, Jethro put on a shirt to eat goose with you. Then off we go a-riding. Jethro taking you a-riding. Your boy, Jethro.'

They swayed in rhythm on the high board seat while the fenderless, cableless vehicle drew them back between the barren fields to her house. The morning-glories were blue under the yellow sky, and the house, inside, was cool. The devil's like a man, she thought, as she set the table. Jethro whistled through the house, walked to the garden, drank from the gourd at the well. She hid away the wax devil so he wouldn't see. She would humor him by day and melt him at night.

But when the meal was over, Jethro set to work. In growing fear, she watched. Out went chairs and table, onto the bed of the truck. Down came the bed in pieces. Her dishes he packed in straw and put in the rain barrel and hoisted up. He laughed and whistled and stopped now and then to pat her where she stood huddled in the corner of the house, watching. 'Don't fret, Old Momma. This here ain't no borried machine. Hit's ourn. Old fool he give it to me for two ten-dollar bills. That don't even make a dent, Old Momma.' And he threw back his head till she thought his neck might crack and laughed.

In fear she watched while the stove pipe came down, whoofing soot onto the whitewashed walls. And the stove he set on the truck and tied with ropes, and last, on top, went the mattress, lumped and humped over the lot of her things, while she found herself in a house now as bare as the fields around.

Then she watched him sit on the front steps, roll himself a smoke, and look at the road.

'Jethro got some figgering to do, Old Momma,' he said, and laughed suddenly. 'For we gone to New Awleens.' He looked at her, pleasure running like water on his face. 'We gone to New Awleens. Gone to the fish country. Get us a house on stilts where the water rock us to sleep at night.' Then, looking at the road, he took up a switch from the yard and drew in the sand.

'How we going though? Valley way's a long way. But take to them hills, we'd be in Alabam.'

Then he argued with himself, while she stood in the door and watched his face work.

'Th'oo the hills? What you saying, boy? That tin can blow its top, man, you knows that. Valley way's the way to go.'

Hill's the quickes' though.

'Hill road bumpy. You got no spare. Rain in the hills. You got no tarp.'

The old woman stole out behind him, but he swung

around and thrust a finger at her. 'Don't you be ugly. Give Jethro a chancet to figger.'

She backed into the dark of the door and stood watching him talk to himself.

'Night catch us in the mountain, we in trouble. You know that. What you thinking? Hurry's what cotch a man, do him in. Be smaht, Jethro. Sun don't set on a nigger in the hills. Hill folks mean folks, you know that.'

He turned and studied her. 'What you think, Momma? Don't you fret. You good luck to Jethro.' Then he looked at the hills rising blue across the valley. 'Take yo' time, boy. New Awleens ain' gone run off. Hit'll wait on you.'

But cross them hills we'd be in Alabam.

'You ain' crossing them hills. Night catch you up there you wish it hadn't. Valley way's the way to go.'

Mountain's the quickes'.

'You know better.'

Whatchoo talkin' bout?

'Sun don't set——'

Who you fraid of?

'Nothin',' he said. 'Nobody!' And he reared back, reaching for her without turning, his eyes set on the hills.

'Come long, Momma.' He eased her forward. As he led her from her empty house, she felt her lips begin to move.

'I cain' make out what you say, Momma.' He was

hoisting her high to the seat of the truck that looked now like a stepped-on bug trailing its injured shell. He fussed behind her and arranged the foot of the mattress to her back so she could lean in comfort.

Her lips moved.

'Just you don't fret. Water's a-coming to this land again. Jethro built the dam and now he take care of Old Momma. Just you don't fret no more,' he sang, 'for we gone to New Awleens.'

The motor strained and coughed and sputtered through the afternoon, winding them along the road, following it into the hills. The devil's a fool, she thought when they kept on rising. Dust hung like a mist over the valley. But they climbed above it. Now and then Jethro stopped to let the radiator cool, and he poured in water from the stream that rushed down the ditch alongside the road. The valley spread before them. Jethro's arm went out.

'Looky there. Ain't it pretty!'

She knew. He offered her the earth and all thereon. She would not look. She would not have it.

And again they climbed. They passed a house and then another further on. A mountain man came out in the road. They looked straight in front of them and Jethro leaned over the high wheel, straining ahead. For the menacing mountain man, he shouted over the din of the motor, 'We be's in Alabam by dark, Old Momma.'

The road grew rocky and the truck backfired on the level stretches. Once, in the forest beside the road, a black bear ambled away from them down the mountainside.

'He goin' fishing,' Jethro said.

As they climbed, the old woman's ears began to sing. Her head grew light and she began to tremble. It was as if at any minute sound too great to bear might roll back the stones from her ears and she might hear.

They rounded a bend in the road and Jethro had to halt and heave a boulder down the mountain so they could pass. Then they went on. Not since first the pebbles lodged in her ears had the old woman been so conscious of stillness. It was as if but a moment before she had heard all sound and now suddenly stillness lay over everything, swelling her head with emptiness light as a bubble. She breathed deep but could not suck in enough air to fill all that vacancy. And like an ant on a drilling bit, the old truck turned and climbed.

High in the hills a fog hung low, but they climbed through it. Then they felt the first big drops of rain.

'Oh-oh,' Jethro said. 'Rain hit's a-coming and we got no tarp.' He yanked the brake and studied the sky. 'We sure nuff in the rain country. It's a-coming.'

A wagon track led off the road, and through the trees they could see a rusty roof. Jethro cut the motor and sat listening to the big, single drops spattering the leaves. He leaped down. She watched him steal out of sight through the woods. Then he came running back.

'Hit's a barn. Hit's empty,' he shouted. She hunched low on the seat, afraid, as Jethro drove them through the underbrush. All that was left of the tumbledown barn was two sides and a roof. And in the clearing beyond, a chimney rose and the rock piles of a burned-down house still made the corners of a square. He drove straight into the barn, and they waited there while the sheets of rain came slanting down like curtains at the open ends.

The air grew cool and smelled of green. And the deep leaf mold sopped the rain. When it stopped, as suddenly as it had started, the sky was clear but purple, and the sun was low.

Jethro climbed down off the seat and walked about the clearing. 'Night done got us,' he mumbled, kicking down a pile of foundation stones. 'Maybe the brakes ain't wet, but that junk heap got no lights on head or tail. Bes' we sit still and wait till morning 'fore we slide down that other side.' He reared back his shoulders and sighed.

The old woman sat high on the seat, her head in the rafters of the barn, pleased that the Lord had sent His sign to halt the devil in his crazy ride.

Jethro reached up and caught her under her armpits and set her down. 'I fix you a bed directly,' he said. 'Don't fret.'

'Now,' he said, seeing her settled on the running board. 'Jethro gone get some dinner. Here's what we do. Heah that waterfall? River's not far off.' He pointed through the dripping leaves. 'Jethro catch us fish for supper. Then he rolls it in mud and builds a fire right here inside where it's dry. We the only ones. We has this whole mountaintop to ourselves. We be's all right till morning.' He glanced behind him toward the road, straightened and pulled up his shoulders and sighed. 'Jethro goin' fishing,' he said.

The old woman's eyes darted, following his hand as it went to his pocket. He brought out a snarled fish line.

'Just a fish line,' he said, holding it out to show her.

She crouched down while he passed by her. He'd begun to whistle, she could tell from his puckered lips as he strode off down a tangled path away from the clearing. She sat where she was till he'd disappeared into the wet and dripping underbrush.

She felt light. Any minute, she thought, she might turn upside down and flop about, banging against the walls and the roof, like the goose flopped after he'd got his hands on it.

She waited another moment, steadying herself, after he'd gone. Then she made her way into the clearing.

She followed the path he'd taken, going stealthily as she could without hearing the sound her footfall made. Rain dripped from the leaves onto her head. She was watching her feet on the slippery path, bent over as she stole her way, her fingers busy freeing her skirts from the clutch of branches, when the sudden fierce light of the sun's dying poured over her. She lifted her face. There before her stretched away the earth. She was standing on the world's top and it spun below, where the waters, swollen with rain, gushed into a chasm. The sight filled her head with sound. The waters rushed, white as milk, over the falls and churned in a vortex at the bottom of the gorge. And, a speck on the ledge above where the path emerged, Jethro wound his stout line about his wrist, tested it, and cast it down.

The old woman, down now on all fours, watched it fall. The cork bobbed, then settled in a rock-walled pool aside from the broiling spectacle. Across the gulf a boulder fell, a rain of pebbles following. Her ears swelled and she thought she must hear.

Above her, on the splinter of ledge that thrust out over the chasm, Jethro leaned out, watching his line, whistling into the fury as he turned the reel of his wrist.

The old woman saw the line dangling before her. She crept forward. It swayed just out of reach beyond the land's end. She waited. Above, Jethro flexed his bound wrist and tested. The line swerved landward, rising. She leaned out and looked from the dizzying height. A silver fillet of fish danced on the hook. She watched it rise until she thought she could grab it. At her touch, the fish fell, plunging back against the gray wall of water where she lost sight of it. But the empty hook blew toward her and she grabbed again.

Her fist closed over her punctured palm, the buried barb. Unbalanced, she clung to the pain she held in her hand and, spinning, saw Jethro's face above, his fixed smile a thing freezing before imminent danger. Her weight, teetering, fell on the line. The shadow of the devil crossed her face as he plummeted. He was hers. She leaned to see him fall, a rag doll flailing.

Then the pain burst with the weight of him in her hand. She felt herself light and spinning, stretched and buffeted. She thought, so this the way it is.

THE BUFFALO FARM

THE signs out front faced down the highway, lettered on both sides so they could be read from either direction, east or west. WESTERN CURIOS—INDIAN JEWELRY—GOOD GRADE GAS—CLEAN REST ROOMS—ICE WATER—FREE ZOO. One, confronting only the westbound cars, warned LAST CHANCE. Across the roof, the name of the place in individual wooden letters, some of which the wind had knocked down to lie bleaching on the shingles. What was left read B F ALO F RM.

The building, a long flat-roofed adobe structure, was flanked on the east by the Clean Rest Rooms and a tire rack—though the tires, New and Used, stood in precarious piles on the ground—and on the west by the buffalo pen, a solid fence of upended poles which, along with the slits for viewing, suggested that the two dusty, woolly, ancient and flea-bitten cows, whatever their appearance, were really dangerous. Out front, two gasoline pumps like armless Indians guarded the stuffed grizzly and the pinto pony humped in the shape of its own rebellion and caught forever, like the mastodon in ice, before which tourists could have their pictures taken. To the north, at some distance across the desert, the mountains rose, first the yellow hills and, behind them, peaks blue in their own shadow.

The dark low-raftered interior, lined with Indian rugs and blankets imported from a factory in upstate New York, offered careless counters of turquoise or polished stone or petrified wood in silver—rings, buckles, bracelets, necklaces—a shelf of cochina dolls and felt moccasins, untidy stacks of Western shirts and skirts, denim levis, cowboy hats, a row of Coca-Cola machine, cigarette machine, chewing gum balls and peanut dispensers, piñon nuts, and peanut butter or cheese in stale cracker sandwiches—four to a Cellophane pack, one nickel. Through the curtained door, the Free Zoo—a Gila monster and a rattler in separate aquariums, one ragged coyote in a wire cage, an eagle and a road runner, both of these stuffed and dusty, with little agate eyes. In the three back rooms Jimmy lived with her husband, Burt the Trader, who was at this moment out behind the kitchen concentrating upon the lettering of two new signs, the tip of his tongue showing like a little pink bullet between his lips. He had already finished one of the signs and stood it up to dry against the adobe wall, where each letter was slowly developing a stinger. It read DON'T MISS THE ATOM BOMB. The other, the one he labored over, said BIG BLAST SEE IT HERE.

31

In the morning, fresh from a night in some ranch-type motel, tourists stopped from both directions. They bought postcards and scribbled on them and put them into purses where they would forget to mail them, bought turquoise rings and silver buckles, took their children through the Zoo, snapped pictures of each other fighting the grizzly or of Junior riding the bucking bronco, peered in at the languishing buffalos, and sampled piñon nuts while spreading maps on fenders, though the road was there, visible for miles in either direction, plainly offering but one choice, unless they wanted to go back where they came from.

But in the afternoon, the cars that stopped in their hurry toward some less lonesome spot before night, stopped only for gasoline if they were heading east, or for nose bags for their radiators if they were heading west into the desert.

Now it was almost night.

Jimmy was standing in the kitchen door, watching her husband work on the signs. She had long ago decided he was mad and the only thing to do was humor him.

She was twenty-two years old and looked to be fifteen, with an undersized body that was all bone. She had on one of her husband's shirts and a pair of black pants stitched up the sides and around the pockets with thread that had once been white. Her yellow straw hair hung straight with an open-end square cut out of it for her face, long and sharp and green-eyed. Her name was really Jimel, after her father and mother, Jim and Elda, back in East Tennessee.

She had been seventeen years old when she married him. He'd told her he was going overseas and was sure to be killed. And then, he said, she would be rich. But she hadn't married him because of the insurance, though she did not at the time doubt that he would be killed if he said so. She had married him because he promised to take her to Florida on their honeymoon. She'd been a little disappointed in everything but the ocean.

In less than a year he was back, but put in an army hospital. He wrote letters saying he'd got a spotty lung and would probably die. But again he didn't. When they released him, they said he would stay cured as long as he lived in some desert. So he'd left the hospital and got on a bus and headed west to find himself a desert, and he'd found The Buffalo Farm and sent for her. By then, she couldn't remember exactly what he looked like.

When she got off the bus she was looking for a short, pale-haired fellow in a damp uniform. But it was a little man in cowboy boots and hat, wearing levis and a bright fuschia corrugated nylon shirt, who grabbed her, kissing. He'd worn the cowboy hat indoors and out, even while he stepped out of his pants at night to go to bed. But she'd soon discovered anyway that, except for the fringe around the edges and a soft yellow down on top, he'd turned bald as an infant.

For a while he entertained her with stories about his experiences in the armed forces. He told her about going out on patrol in no man's land, and about the stink of dead bodies, and about a crazy Chinese radio that blared out propaganda to them at night and played American jazz music on what sounded like kitchen utensils. And he told her about Japanese women when he was on leave, making out that he'd been quite a heller. But then she was wakened one night by his sobs and he confessed that he'd never seen a Chinese soldier, never been on patrol, that the only stink he'd come in contact with was in the latrines. He'd spent his months in Korea with a reserve battalion near a place he called Sayool, and that was where they discovered his spotty lung. From then on he'd been in the hospital. The two letters he'd written to her were full of nothing but lies.

After that she got to know him better because he talked about what was really on his mind. He talked about his death. His death was like a ribbon-tied box he kept in front of him all the time. He didn't know what was in it for him and he wouldn't have dared to touch the ribbon. But nevertheless he kept it always before him, at arm's length, where he could look at it and talk about it and be reminded by it that he was set apart from other men. It was his obsession, that and making money. He said he hadn't long to live and he wanted to make a lot of money before he died.

Squatting before his sign, Burt asked, 'What do you think? Is two enough?'

Jimmy didn't answer. She was thinking about the ocean. Though she had seen it only on that one occasion in her life, she found it was a good deal more real to her than anything she remembered from East Tennessee. (Mountains made her car sick.) She had found that looking at the desert made it easier for her to conjure up the ocean, a thing she was likely to do in time of stress. She thought it helped to look at the desert because it was just so much nothing and didn't intrude upon her mind. So, standing there at the back door, she looked out across the arroyo and the sand flats to the mesa and, beyond, to the mountains, and the ocean suddenly loomed up, blue with white sand beaches, seeming to rise toward the distances, so big it was like something you try to get your hands on in a dream. Her eyes glazed over with the look of one hypnotized, or dead. It made her feel the way she had upon inhaling her first cigarette as a child, full and lightheaded and gone from this world.

It lasted only an instant, and afterwards there was only the arroyo where rested the wind-sanded, rusting-out carcass of the old wreck Burt had pushed down there with his jeep, and clumps of mesquite, and a distant butte that looked like a man buried in sand up to his neck, and the desert itself that remained to mock her, a gross personal insult.

She turned her eyes back upon her husband. 'Sometimes I think you hadn't got a lick of sense,' she said.

He smiled up at her and went on with his work.

35

He had finished both signs and now was getting ready to nail them onto posts. 'You want to help me with this now?' he asked. 'I got to get busy on them sun glasses. There's a world of things to be done yet.'

He stood up and took off his hat and fanned himself. She slammed out into the yard and took hold of one of the signposts. She looked at his bald head. She hadn't often an opportunity to see it. The ridge the hat made cut across his forehead like a scar. Above it his head was unnaturally white, while below, his nose and cheeks were peeling and red, and his eyebrows and lashes were bleached. His taking off his hat was a testimonial to his excitement.

'What are you going to do with the sun glasses?' she asked, still studying the scar the hat made. He'd come home that morning from a quick trip up the highway and into the nearest town loaded down with cardboard boxes stuffed full of 29¢ and 59¢ and 69¢ sun glasses. He'd bought out every drug store and dime store and trading post for twenty miles to the east.

'I aim to add one dollar in front of each and every one of those prices,' he said.

'They prob'ly won't even need them to see it,' she said.

'Well, they won't *know* that till it's all over,' he said. 'By then I'll have made a fortune.' He picked up his hammer and began to drive nails while she braced her shoulder against the back of the post. He'd made lots of fortunes before. Once he'd made Julia Crow, their Indian help, take him out into the desert. He'd taken hundreds of color slides of buttes and cactus and one old Indian ruin. He'd sold one of the pictures to a postcard company. And once he'd bought six burros, planning to take pack trips out toward the mountains, charging tourists some outrageous prices. He never could make a go of that though, and he blamed it on the fact they didn't have a motel where tourists could stay and get an early start in the mornings. So he'd built a ring and hired out the burros for kiddie rides until they all got choked one spring in a sand storm.

Every blow of the hammer knocked her teeth together. 'Hurry up, will you please,' she said. 'It'll be here by the time you get these things up.'

'Hold your horses. I'm almost through.'

Whack, and she felt a crick coming in her neck. But he'd finished.

He picked up his mallet and leaned on it to survey his handiwork. 'In the morning,' he said, 'I expect to see cars lining as far as you can see on both sides of the highway.'

'How do you know so sure you'll even be able to see it from here?' she asked. But he ignored her.

'Dropped two on Japan and they flattened a city apiece.' He snapped his fingers. 'Just like that.' Now he had stuck the handle of the mallet into the sand and was sitting on its head, rolling a smoke.

He started to go on, but his eyes shifted and he looked down at what he was doing. She saw that he'd been about to describe the cities as if he'd seen both of them. She knew that sometimes he could have kicked himself for confessing to her about his war experiences that night he woke up dreaming about his birthday box of death.

He went on. 'Millions of 'em, dead before they knew what hit um, cinders in a second.' He stuck the cigarette between his lips and searched his pockets for a match to light it. 'You take most of them, why they'd never even thought about it.' Snap. 'Out like a light. None of your little crossroads bus stops either, big cities the size of L.A.' Snap.

Jimmy balanced the sign and tried to wipe a smear of paint off her temple.

He shook his head, smiling a little. 'You couldn't of paid me to been in one of them.'

'When I die I want it to be quick,' she said.

'Take I read where they dropped one of them on this island. They were just trying it out. Put all these sheep and goats in crates and leftum there to see what effect it would have. Why, baby, when it was all over, know what? There wasn't even an island. That's what effect it had.' He chuckled. 'Sometimes they don't get it set just like they want it.'

Julia Crow waddled around the end of the buffalo pen to see what they were doing. Julia Crow came once a week, bringing moccasins and cochina dolls off the reservation. And she stayed the day to clean up and cook supper for them. For this Burt paid her two dollars over the price of her wares, most of which he shipped east at a five hundred per cent profit to his brother who ran a trading post in the Smoky Mountains, where the 'Navaho Handicraft' was re-labeled 'Cherokee Curios' and sold along with chenille bedspreads. She was a fat dark Indian woman with little eyes like raisins in a burnt roll, and she had come that morning waddling out of the desert with two sacks of souvenirs tied into the ends of her shawl and slung forward over her shoulders to form a pair of breasts in no way out of proportion to the rest of her. In the course of the morning, posed between the stuffed grizzly and the pinto pony, she had contrived to have her picture taken many times. She always posed with arms crossed under her shawl, grim-faced, her large lips stretched to cover her larger teeth, but she broke into helpless giggles afterwards, holding out her palm. At this the tourists were likely to look hurt or to doubt Julia's authenticity. Half of the tourists came determined to believe everything. The other half were just as determined to believe nothing, and they picked over the items for sale, murmuring, 'Made in Japan.'

Burt had talked Julia Crow into staying and helping out with the mob he expected to converge upon The Buffalo Farm before dawn. Now as she waddled up to them, he let the cigarette dangle from the corner of his lips and trail a thread of smoke that made his eye water. The sight of Julia Crow had somewhat the same settling effect on him that the vision of the ocean had on his wife. He studied her with a fixed and

39

distant look, for she was the one Indian they had gotten on terms with, and he felt that there was something to be done with her if he could just think what. The fact that she was alive increased her value, but at the same time made her uses difficult to settle on. But far from being frustrated by the challenge she represented, each time he looked at her he was kindled to dreams out of all proportion to the Free Zoo and the buffalo pen. Someday it would come to him. In the meantime he encouraged her visits and treated her with deference.

'Whadayuh think, Julia?' he asked. 'Whadayuh think will happen when the bomb goes off?' Her silence fascinated him and led him to believe that if he could but get her to talk, the revelation he was after might spring balloon-shaped from her lips. So he was forever asking her foolish questions.

'Make a boom-boom,' she said, with a grin that squeezed the raisin eyes almost out of sight.

He gazed at her, letting the words settle like rolling dice so he could read them and sift their meaning.

'What do *you* think is going to happen?' Jimmy asked, a suspicion too big to grasp circling over her consciousness.

He laughed. 'I think we going to make us a killing.'

Julia Crow chuckled and Burt's eyes jumped to her face. 'Ain't that right, Julia?'

'Big killing,' she agreed.

'You think,' Jimmy said, speaking as she might have in a dream, or hypnotized. 'You think maybe they won't get it set just right in the morning, don't you. You think we might all of us get blown sky-high. You plan on selling all those sun glasses at three hundred per cent profit to a bunch of people without long on this earth, don't you. And that's how come you're laughing under your hat, idn't it.'

He chuckled. 'Whadayuh think, Julia? We going to get blown up or what?'

Julia Crow raised her arms slowly into a circle and pursed her lips. 'Posh!' she said.

Burt was visibly shaken. The cigarette trembled in his lips and he didn't take his eyes off her.

Jimmy let go the sign and it arched over to slap the ground and send up a little spurt of alkali. 'Listen. If there's a chance in a million that'll happen, I'm high-tailing it out of here.'

'Now cahm down,' Burt said. 'Just cahm down. I'm going to need me all the help I can get here in the morning. Anyway—' he dropped the cigarette and put his foot on it '—they know what they're doing.'

'They blew up that island without meaning to.'

'They had more experience at it now.'

Julia Crow giggled, looking from one of them to the other, folding her arms underneath her shawl.

Burt rolled another cigarette, licked it sealed with a flamboyant swipe of his tongue, stuck it in his mouth, and searched his pockets again for a match. 'What if they did?' he said. 'And we got buried in the sand from it and they dug us up two thoud'n years from now. Take they found this place just like it is tonight and

41

you and me and Julia—' he turned his mystical white gaze upon the Indian—'you and me and Julia all mummified to a fare-you-well.'

'You said they went up in cinders,' Jimmy said.

He shrugged, lighting his match. 'Happens all kind of ways.'

'Shoot,' Jimmy said, 'If you thought that was what was going to happen, you'd hitch a ride out of here on a motorcycle and we'd of seen the last of you.'

'Whadayuh think, Julia?' he asked.

Julia Crow shook like Santy Claus, chuckling silently in her wisdom.

In the desert at night the stars hang low, suspended from a bent black sky, like Christmas baubles in a fir, just out of reach. And people and the walls they build around small spaces seem shrunken from their due proportions, the lighted ceiling of air and walls of mountains like sleeping dinosaurs. And there are no anachronisms unless time itself is upside down and man awakes and squints and lifts his meager self from tomb and pyramid to find the earth no longer his.

But a lecturer at the Grand Canyon said, Take this ditch and imagine on its rim a needle standing on its head, and take this to be a picture of the history of earth, and the needle is the history of man, infinitesimal upon the ages.

And Jimmy had wandered to the edge to see how far down she could spit. Not far, for the wind took the spittle, whipped it to feathered foam, and dispersed it in the air. The river at the bottom was a metallic thread, too thin to have sawed away all this, no mightier than the needle standing on its head and meant to be a man. She didn't for a minute believe that pitch.

And then the Indians in fancy costumes had danced on a stage the size of a drum. She'd thought of Julia Crow and spit again.

Now cars were beginning to spread out along the shoulders of the highway and into the desert itself, their headlights criss-crossed ribbons on the sand. It was three hours past midnight. Burt was doing a lively trade in trinkets out front. Cochina dolls and Coca-Colas went like hotcakes, and voices melted into pools inside the Zoo where the sleepy coyote circled in his cage and the rattler bruised his forked tongue against the glass and the eagle's agate eyes looked haughtily out across the sea of heads. And Julia Crow smiled and smiled and spoke no Englis', except to make change.

Jimmy wandered out of the trading post, past the buffalo pen where one restive cow mounted the other, and into the dip of the arroyo where she almost stepped on a pair of lovers wrestling in the sand. She turned and wandered toward the butte.

A pickup truck had parked with its nose toward the mountains, and a woman sitting in the cab spoke to her. 'Honey, kin I trouble you for a light?'

Jimmy stopped, searched her pockets, and came up with a wooden kitchen match. She stroked it on the rusted hood and held it toward the woman. In its flare she saw a man sprawled against the far door, asleep, with his hat mashed against the back of the seat, and a woman as old as her mother giving suck to a wrinkled, elderly-looking baby.

She held the match to the cigarette drooping from the woman's mouth, and the woman, like the infant, sucked away.

'Thanks a lot, honey. What time's it getting to be?'

Jimmy shrugged and walked on, parallel now to the highway, through the populated desert. A circle of Indian men gambled with dice on the bed of a truck, throwing the bones against the backboard, snapping fingers and cursing. 'Hot damn, Little Joe. Sweet Jesus!'

'It is my feeling,' she heard a man say to a small group of people gathered around the hood of a station wagon like a family at dinner, 'that we have crossed this country to find only another ocean. No frontiers are left to us and here we are, beached on the desert with no place left to go, unless it's up and we explore the universe itself.'

'Go up in smoke!' a second man said.

The first man, a black silhouette with only its face illuminated, nodded. 'That may be,' he said. 'It's a chance we have to take.'

Another one said softly, 'There is the soul. Always the soul that will be there waiting, its mystery unsolved, when all the worlds are known and all the beasts put down.'

The second man said, 'It's a bomb, not a space ship.'

And they thought about that.

She moved away.

All the cars had their radios going, and the voice of the radio explaining what would happen sounded like that of a solemn priest putting out exciting things in a language no one could understand any more. Everywhere she went, the same low sexless voice was there ahead of her, making it seem as though she stood still, going no place.

A man said to a woman, 'The way I look at it, we *got* this thing. How come they want to outlaw it? It's all killing. Might just as well be expert about it. The trouble with them is they think it's a game you play by a set of rules. They make up rules and set up men like checkers on a board, different colors and you can't jump backwards and all that. But this thing! It's too big to play with. It'll ruin their war games. That's how come they want to outlaw it.'

'I don't follow you,' the woman said. 'Women just don't understand the way you men think.'

'Balls,' Jimmy said. They turned to look at her, and she walked away.

Two students were down on their knees in the blare of headlights. One had a stick and was drawing in the sand. 'Now here's the structure of the uranium atom,' he said. 'And the bombardment works—wait a minute. Now look at this, will you . . .'

A girl in horn-rimmed glasses said to the slender young man sitting on the blanket beside her, 'What a story! I think this will sell. Listen.' She raised a hand as if visualizing or drawing in the air the scene she described. 'The world's just heard the news—the bomb's been outlawed, stock piles all destroyed, disarmament has begun. Everything's at fever pitch. People jubilant. Parades in every street. Like the Elizabethans. Start at some peak of perfection and there's no place to go but down. Here's the gimmick. *Marvelous* irony. Comes the dawn. It's all *too late*. Scientists discover that radiation has already gone beyond the limit. Ta-da. Music. Quick contrast. People weeping. Dejected. The whole world's been sterilized, see. Get in a Biblical twist. That's always good. First the fishes die off, then the fowl, etcetera. Mankind's only hope for survival lies in the possibility that the embryos in the wombs all over the world might still be potent. All the women in a family way become the property of the state and have to go to hospitals underground to insure every precaution against radiation.

'Look at the possibilities for vignettes! Terrific pathos. Families torn up. Young couples forcibly separated. Say they won't be able to tell until the children reach the age of puberty. I'd have to do a little research. But look at the angles! Economy. What happens there while the world waits? Baby-foods manufacturers going out of business, advertising affected, etcetera. Education! Kindergartens closing down in a few years, then no first grades, no second grades and so on. No grade schools. Then high schools. The whole world at a virtual standstill, waiting. Everything focused on the caves where the new generation is being reared. Get the picture? It's *loaded* with symbols. It's like going back to the beginning, back to the cave men, see. How do they teach these children? What do their little textbooks talk about? Trees? They've never seen a tree. Animals? They've all died off. Everyone's a vegetarian. And morals! What happens to morals?'

The young man threw himself into it, stretching out his long legs onto the sand and leaning on one elbow. 'I think the morals should go to pot. Interesting. Would sex without procreation really become meaningless? It would raise questions. Show the Pope in conclave with his cardinals trying to figure out an encyclical on *that* one. Possibilities for humor there.' He whooped with laughter. 'Anyway, you could use it to advantage. Juice it up a bit. Make it sell. The whole world in an orgy of escape!'

'Terrific! And mankind in the balance, looking toward a generation of children growing up like moles in caves. What kind of civilization would they make, I wonder?'

'After the orgy, I suspect there'd be a religious revival,' he said.

'There's a gimmick! Get in some intellectual content. And I think it might just end like the lady and the tiger. People on their knees in the streets, waiting

47

to hear loud speakers announce the results of the tests on the children. Waiting to hear if mankind has a future!'

'Curtain! I think you've really got something there. Maybe a best seller.'

'I don't know,' she said, sighing. 'It might be a pot boiler. My natural indolence may keep it from being great.'

And together, in silence, they contemplated the awful reality of her natural indolence.

Jimmy came to a spot dark and clear of cars. She squatted on her heels and looked toward the mountains, wondering what time it was. She yawned. She intended to sleep all day when it was over, and Burt could hang himself for all she cared. She sat in the sand and took a Hershey bar out of her pocket and peeled back the paper like the skin of a banana.

A voice close to her said, 'Repent, Madam, while yet there's time.' It was a voice with a lot of breath in it.

She sat perfectly still, looking straight ahead of her into the dark.

Then, on feet that fell soundlessly on the sand, a form moved very close to her. She turned. A man in outline darker than the night stood towering over her. He let himself down, carefully, as though his bones were dry and brittle things, and he knelt on the ground and put his hands together like a child praying. A car turned off the highway, and before its lights went out she saw his face, gaunt and bony like a death head, shaggy-haired like some desert wolf.

'I will pray with you,' he said.

She held the peeled chocolate while it began to go soft in her fingers. 'Who ast you to?' she said.

'You do not have to ask.'

'Listen, who do you think you are anyway?'

'I am the Christ.'

'Yeah, I thought so,' she said. 'I'm Mary. Pleased-ta-meetcha.'

He gasped and put his face up close to hers until she had to move back from his stinking breath. She didn't smell any liquor on him, though. 'Do not blaspheme,' he said, 'now and in this hour of our death. Come. Let us pray.'

'G'wan, pray if you want to, but leave me alone.'

'Alone—alone. Has it occurred to you, Madam, that I could not do otherwise, that we are all irrevocably alone here as on a darkling plain and it is the cross we must bear? Alone.' He grabbed her hand and folded it against his chest. 'Aye, there's the rub. But look! Isn't it also our human bond? Alone. It is the thing we all of us have in common, that makes us brethren, one with another.'

She turned cautiously to see how far out alone she'd come. The Buffalo Farm shone luminous as a fallen star where Burt had turned on the fluorescent lights over the gas pumps.

'Come,' he said gently. 'Let us pray. There is not a great deal of time.' He held her hand between his own and lifted his head to lay it on the wind. His straggly little goatee fluttered like a tail on a radiator.

49

'Prayer,' he began. 'I have lived my life and that which I have done may He within Himself make pure——'

'What've you done?' she whispered, the hand in his gone numb.

'But thou, if thou shouldst never see my face again——'

'Jesus!' she whispered. 'I hope I never.'

She drew her hand little by little from those of the madman and rolled up on her knees like a football player on the line, her chocolaty hand gathering sand like a tide-deserted anemone. Then she shot up. At the length of her coat tail, she jerked, poised a second, and plopped hard. He had hold of her clothes.

'I am the hound of heaven,' he said. 'Listen.'

She wasn't breathing, and her lungs were swollen like a balloon about to burst.

'Now pray with me,' he said.

'O.K.—O.K., I'll pray with you.' She crouched, looking now toward the highway where a car eased off the ribbon, dipped, and showered the two of them with light as it crept out over the sand.

He had her wrist in the iron ring of his fingers. 'What shall we pray, Sister?'

'Anything. You choose.' The car would reach them in a moment, if it didn't stop first.

'All right,' he said. 'Say after me, "I repent me——" '

'I repent me——'

'Say, "O, my God, I am heartily sorry for all my sins because I dread the loss of heaven and the pains of hell, but most of all because they offend Thee——" '

But he'd let go of her and fallen over to beat his head on the ground.

The car was getting close now. She felt safe. She leaned over the crazy man and saw that he wore a black suit that was threadbare and shiny.

'Listen, get on up. They like to ran over you.'

His muttering continued. He acted as if he no longer knew that she was there.

Now the cars had turned off their headlights and looked like black ants sudden-died there on a flattened hill where some giant had stepped. In the east she saw a candle's glow, faint from under the horizon. People had climbed out of cars and trucks to stand together, silent now, looking toward the mountains over whose summit they expected to see the second coming of the sun. There was no traffic on the highway now, no movement anywhere, and not a sound from the crowd behind them. The wind had died, and she realized it was dawn. In the silence, the voice of the radio said 'Five—four—three—two—'

She poked the lunatic's shoulder with her fingers. 'Get up,' she whispered. 'It's about to happen. Look!'

The sun rose in the north with a curious light, too quick, and the desert was green, and the multitude turned burnt black holes up to the sky. An *Ahhhh* rose up like a prayer they couldn't articulate.

Then the earth began to tremble and there was an instant when it fell away and, like dancers, they hovered in a little leap, and then the ground rose up again.

The uncanny false day came higher, and they stood as if waiting to hear a voice. But the sound that came was like a ghostly locomotive whose rail was the air, the mountains, desert, sky. And a cloud rose up, bigger than the mountain, pink as a sunrise-sunset over the earth at the same instant.

She was kneeling in the sand, in the arms of the lunatic, who turned to the mountain with eyes that put her in mind of something. *The ocean.* His jaw hung down and he said, 'Now.' And she heard it, the suck of the sea receding, and she held on to his coat and looked up at his face.

He patted her back. 'Come. Follow me.'

She rose and stumbled after him where he led her by the hand. He'd turned his back on the mountain. He walked to face the silent mob where a whisper could have been heard, and he stopped before them, holding his arms stretched out.

'I am the resurrection and the light!' he shouted.

She dropped on the ground at his feet, afraid, trying to make herself small, and looked up at his quivering chin with its little fluttering beard.

'Take up thy cross and follow me!'

But in the east the faint day was returning. The sun rose dim and tiny, timid as a child barred from some obscene display, but daring to look, now it was over.

The madman shouted to the hesitating crowd, 'I

am the Alpha and the Omega. Repent! And wash in the blood of the lamb——'

A woman sniggered. And slowly they began to climb into their finned and chromium-plated automobiles. Out in the desert, tires skidded in turns, backed, braked, whipped up sprays of sand.

It was over. They were going. The exodus was slow, a cortege of cars going back to Las Vegas, east, into the timid sun.

The lunatic held out his arms, frozen there like the grizzly and the pony. And Jimmy shivered at his feet.

Then Burt and Julia Crow came from the Buffalo Farm, Burt with his eyes streaming out a flood of tears. Stumbling, blind to the cars that swerved around them, he clung to Julia Crow, his face lifted as if he'd witnessed a private vision.

'He who follows me, though he die, yet will he live,' shouted the lunatic.

Burt put up his head and listened, moving like a blind man in the direction of the voice. Jimmy held on to the man's coat tail and tried to see into his face.

'I am the everlasting. If a seed fall into the earth and die, then and only then shall it live!'

'Did you see it? Did you see?' Burt said, his voice ecstatic.

The man turned toward the pair. 'Come,' he said, sighing, taking Julia Crow by the hand. 'Be my hand-maiden. Follow me.'

Julia Crow hung back, giggling.

'Come,' the man said again, and fickle Julia Crow, still giggling, followed him toward the highway.

'No!' Burt shouted, trotting after them, catching hold of Julia's shawl. Jimmy grasped the man's bony arm and set her heels in the sand.

'No,' Burt shouted. 'Look. Don't go!' He ran his sleeve under his nose and rubbed his fists in his eyes. 'Stay here. There's going to be more of them. Stay!'

The man turned slowly, looked at Jimmy and Burt, then at the mountain. He shook his head. 'I must be about my father's business,' he said.

'We got *plenty* of business,' Burt said. He had hold of Julia Crow's arm and was turning them back toward the Buffalo Farm. The man surveyed the place with his sunken eyes.

Jimmy whispered, touching his arm, 'Have a Coca-Cola.'

The man walked up to the buffalo pen. 'It is the ark,' he said, pausing to look at the sleeping animals. 'It is the ark and we will make a covenant.'

'Yeah,' Burt said eagerly, clinging to Julia Crow. 'We'll build us a covenant right over there for you, a real old-fashioned pioneer covenant with a pair of stuffed oxes to pull it and Indian arrows sticking in the canvas and I know where we can get us some wagon wheels.'

'Two by two,' the man said, taking Julia Crow's hand. 'We will go into it two by two and await the subsiding of the waters and the return of the dove.'

'We'll *get* some,' Burt said.

And together they entered the building by way of the Zoo. The coyote blinked a sleepy eye at them and the rattler bruised his tongue against the glass, and the agate eyes of the bird looked over their heads.

A SIMPLE CASE

IN THE last half of August when the days begin almost imperceptibly to shorten, at around dusk in the Great Plains states the light sometimes gets a blue fall cast to it, and in this blue cast of light when the sun's gone down things take on an unearthly, strange appearance and one has to look carefully, and look again, to be sure of what he sees. It was, to Harold Widkins, a favorite time, not only because he could freely admit to having quit work for the day, but also because of the light itself that seemed to put things in a kind of distant perspective that rendered life a bit closer to his ideal of it.

When Harold walked from the outdoor light into the dim kitchen, he did not at first believe that he saw, standing with his back turned at the sink, a man peculiarly dressed and wearing a mask. His first impulse was to call his wife, who was in the hen house, to see for herself. For he knew she would never take his word for it.

But before he did anything at all, the masked man

whirled around and grabbed up an oddly shaped gun from beside the cooling pie on the sideboard. It was this action, more than anything else, that convinced Harold Widkins that his eyes, in the blue dusk light, did not deceive him, and he felt a stir of excitement in his breast. He looked from the gun, which he classified as 'foreign made,' to the mask. It was a small black mask such as children wear at Halloween and ladies in the movies wear to gala masked balls. It had little slits in it that made the burglar's eyes look oriental, lidless and surprised, under the wide brim of the black felt hat.

The masked man stood there, an exotic thing in that familiar kitchen, and shook the gun like a finger at Harold. And Harold, in the midst of his fear and surprise, felt something like delight run through him, as though he were not just watching, but taking part in a kind of performance.

The burglar (as Harold designated him) didn't say anything. He kept casting his lidless eyes about the kitchen as if in some confusion as to what came next. And Harold, like a member of an audience watching an actor forget his lines, strained forward a little, as though he would like to prompt the man, toward whom he already felt a kind of proprietorship. He thought, in a momentary disappointment, that the burglar might be looking for a place to hide.

At that instant, Mildred Widkins came in from the hen house and stopped abruptly beside Harold, who had not moved from the door.

'See!' Harold said, as though he intended, 'See, I told you!' His wife's sharp gasp was the final confirmation of the burglar's real presence.

Then the muzzle of the pistol wavered between them as he said, clearly and unmistakably, 'This is it!' The fright in Harold was mixed with a kind of satisfaction at the rightness of the expression.

Then the gun steadied, its aim coming to rest on Harold, singling him out. In the pure and empty silence, they heard the loud *click*!

For the first time, Harold moved. He drew open the long drawer in the silver chest beside him on the cabinet, took out his own .38, and turned back in time to see the other man's finger squeeze again.

Harold fired.

The bullet hit the burglar below the left eye, just under the mask, and he fell back with the impact against the sink and slithered slowly to the floor where he sat, dead, propped against the plumbing.

Harold stood looking down at him, feeling, in spite of the accuracy of his shot, in some vague way disappointed. He tiptoed across the bright linoleum as if the man were asleep and bent from the waist to look down at the burglar's face. The left eye was becoming bloodshot, but the right one stared back at Harold in a kind of conspiracy. It was, Harold saw, a blue eye, and that came as a shock to him. Below the mask the cheeks were shaven and unmarked except for the clean hole of the bullet. Harold stroked his whiskers and noted the sand color of the sideburns that showed, long and curved, beneath the black felt hat that was still set firmly down on the burglar's head.

Then Harold understood his reason for thinking the man was peculiarly dressed. He was wearing a dark suit of winter clothes on a day when the temperature at noon had gone well over a hundred degrees in the shade.

As he bent there over his victim, Harold seemed to hear his own voice telling the story to an audience indistinct but large, pausing for weight while his hands gestured effectively. Then he saw it as if it were on a screen and he could watch himself. He had grown taller and was wearing boots. The gun, when he whipped it out, came from a holster on his hip, and the woman he swept behind him was Mildred as she had been when first he courted her. In the picture he was as obviously a hero as the burglar, in reality, was obviously a burglar.

Mildred Widkins, her chafed fingers held tightly to her mouth, crept up beside her husband, and together, in silence, for another moment they looked down. Then she removed her fingers from her mouth and whispered, 'Don't touch anything. They tell you not to go touching everything.'

'I ain't laid a hand on him,' Harold said in a loud, argumentative voice.

'Look there!' she said, her voice little more than a whisper.

He looked where she was pointing. The man's right hand, open but with the gun lying loosely on his palm, was missing the tip of its index finger.

'I seen that,' Harold lied.

'You never no-such-of-a-thing,' his wife said.

But Harold had come to feel so full of an inexplicable sadness that he didn't answer her back. He thought it was because Mildred had a natural capacity for spoiling things.

Harold Widkins was a straggle-haired man with a long trunk and exceptionally short legs. His mouth had deep creases enclosing it on either side like parentheses, and his eyebrows were perpetually raised, as though the whole of his life had been a surprising disappointment.

He was a man who had secretly always waited for something extraordinary to happen to him—love at first sight, discovery of buried treasure, guerilla warfare, the ability to speak in tongues, wild public acclaim—anything to lift up his life and give it the kind of reality he had, even as a boy, come to expect. He had always loved a circus or a parade. When circuses and parades came to be all but extinct, he attended, in place of them, several auction sales a week. He had not in his younger years missed a single movie that had come to the Picture Palace in Grand Junction, and his house was the first on that rural route to display, amid anachronistic lightning rods, the aluminum cross that heralded the awesome mystery of television. So Harold knew very well how life ought to be.

The trouble with life, he had often felt, was that you never had any practice for the big things, and that was why it was so easy to make a fool of yourself. When his father died he hadn't known how to act, though it had seemed to him that everybody else knew very well. He thought it must have been because he was young at the time. The others were older and had gone through it all before. Harold had made a fool of himself by weeping, until an uncle had pointed out to him that tears were womanish. And then he'd taken it into his head to talk. He didn't seem to be able to stop talking, so the same uncle had been forced to hit him across the face in order to make him act in a more seemly fashion. He envied the burglar his rightness in all that he had done, for he himself had never been able to carry off a big moment, not that there'd been many such opportunities in his life.

For one thing, he usually talked too much for a man. At mealtime, while the women—his wife and sister-in-law—ate, silent, their eyes on their plates, Harold would talk about his 'quipment,' about the new heavy tractor he planned to trade for, and how if he'd had a corn picker he could have made 'several thoud'n dollars' on corn. The truth was, Harold had, here and there about the farm, two tractors, a baler, a mower, a wagon, two rakes, miscellaneous attachments—plows, disks, cultivators—not all of them completely paid for and at least half of them out of commission in some way and of the other half at least one or two big pieces that, if the truth were known, Harold either did not know how to operate or was afraid of. One tractor had been parked out of sight behind the barn since a year ago last May. It had a broken motor, and once broken, a motor was of no use to him thereafter. For, to Harold, a motor was as much of a mystery as the workings of the government. But he could talk about both in a know-ledgeable way to the womenfolk.

'Cylinder's busted,' he would say. 'Take a hunnert dollars to fix it.' Or, 'Long's them dang Reds are in the White House, the farmer's gone to suffer. No use to talk about it. Take a hunnert thoud'n dollars to make a dime the way things are.' So Mrs. Widkins raised fryers and hens, fattened calves and butchered hogs and sold her butter.

Harold was actually a wise man, but he didn't trust his wisdom. He knew, for instance, that he talked too much and in figures too extravagant, and that people distrust a man who talks overmuch. He knew that his father had been a drinker, had beaten the children, had not been above taking a hand to his wife. But his father had been a silent man, and people all woke up and took notice when he spoke his meager words. He could say, 'Rain tonight,' and if the sky stayed clear they thought the Lord had made an oversight.

Harold knew as a child that he'd never be as big a

man as his father, and his growth had borne him out. It wasn't that he was really a smaller man. In his chest and arms and back he was as strong and as big as his father had ever been. It was just that his legs were so stumpy. He realized, in his wisdom, that if he hadn't taken the time to explain it, they might all have seen this for themselves. But he would go ahead and explain it, time and again. He'd make up his mind in the morning to start holding his tongue, but by noon something would have to be explained, so talk he would, and see the guarded, polite faces. Or he'd hold his tongue awhile, hoping that his wife or his sister-in-law would speak up for him, tell them that he worked hard, that he tried, did the best he could, that his father had sons to help while he had none, that his father lived before there was 'quipment' to cope with, and the 'govermunt' and the drought. But the women never did speak up for him, so, explaining himself to polite faces, he would know the anguish of the lonely in defense of themselves.

He longed for a team to talk to. Who could talk to a sputtering tractor? He longed for a dog to follow him about from one chore to the next, but the pups, despite his coaxing, always stayed close to the kitchen waiting for a handout. Then, insulted by their indifference and to salvage his pride, he further alienated them by abuse.

He didn't have a way with animals like his father'd had, or a green thumb with crops, or the favor of the Almighty in the weather. Old Sam Widkins had always prayed the blessing at meals, spoke right up to God as his equal. But Harold couldn't pray. His wife was a church woman with a thoroughgoing knowledge of righteousness, and she knew his lusts and failures, his weaknesses and his sins. How could he pray with his wife at the table listening?

But Harold was proud of his wife, proud to have got her foolish long enough to win her, proud to have begot two daughters on her. And he would tell over and over how he'd won her, hoping someday to hit on the truth about it. But truth was mixed up in his mind with what ought to have been, with what he wanted to believe, and with what lore and the television preached at him about courtship and love and family life. And Harold tried to hold on to his faith in those things, even though television itself sometimes troubled his peace of mind. For interspersed in half-minutes between the Western heroes, loving mothers, precocious children, kindly, comic fathers, and singing lovers, spaced here and there amid a world that seemed to Harold all that was good, came the commercials appealing to his wisdom. With constricted breast he watched the white-coated man demonstrate the congestion of sinus; saw the silhouette of the human body, the digestive tract suddenly illumined; listened to all the ills of man, saw pills trickle down the diagrammed gullet and fall into the stomach to be rushed to the ailing blood stream, watched the scientific delineation of a headache—a hammer on the skull. Headache, neuralgia, neuritis, the common cold, sinusitis, indigestion, constipation, diarrhea, hemorrhoids, arthritis, tooth decay, bad breath from gastritis, from mouth germs, body odor, piles, rheumatism and its accompanying ills, iron-deficiency anemia, tired blood, acne, broken hair ends, brittle nails, chafed hands, corns, fallen arches, nausea, insomnia, malfunctioning kidney excess fat. And Harold's breathing would come in short gasps as he gripped the arms of his chair and his wisdom tried to respond, to shout, 'True! True! All of it true!'

But then the smiling man came on and told him to rest assured, that science had found a way, a miracle medicine, a pill or lotion, plaster, vapor, ointment, a syrup that not only cured but tasted good as well. This philter, that formula, added to an herb used by the Indians in olden times, and youth perpetual can be yours, Harold Widkins. He seemed so genial, so sure of himself, so kind in what he offered, this latter-day medicine man, that Harold instantly relaxed. And then the music came and on the screen again the hero battled evil in the form of recognizable villains, and always won. Wives honored husbands, children loved parents, and lovers were always true. The day was saved, and with it Harold's faith.

Along with his faith, he had a great deal of hope. He usually whistled in the morning and found good omen in whatever the sky promised, sun or rain. He'd talk at breakfast about all he intended to do that day, and he would eat hearty, for he was still naïve enough to believe that there was no sight softened a woman's heart and temper quicker than the sight of a man gorged on her own cooking. His wife's heart nor temper, either, ever softened. The truth was, she had a frugal bent and a meager appetite herself, and the sight of Harold stuffing himself shocked her sense of decency.

And Harold usually summoned hope again as he came back from the fields at night. He would talk at supper about the world, the farm, the 'quipment', again under the illusion that women like to be instructed, that they felt safer knowing that he knew so much, that they trusted and respected his patience with their natural ignorance. His wisdom told him better, but he did not trust his wisdom, it being so contrary.

In answer to his wife's telephone summons, the sheriff of Grand Junction came squealing down the highway in a patrol car driven by an officer named Hemingway—a large man strapped and belted, with a pistol at his hip, a visored cap, and a pair of black boots that hugged his shapely calves. Behind them, driving his own dusty Ford, came the newspaperman, who took a picture of Harold looking startled by the events that followed one another too fast and by the flash of the camera.

The light of the flash, flaring and dying so suddenly, made the kitchen seem, by contrast, very dim. So

Mildred Widkins reached up and pulled the chain on the bulb that hung naked and free from the ceiling. The light came on, yellow and faint after the white splash of an instant before. And the electric cord swung in a wide arc when she let it go, so that everything seemed to move in the swaying light, even the corpse, though except for the bulb swinging there over their heads nothing really moved at all.

The sheriff asked Harold how the shooting had come about.

'Well,' Harold began, looking from newspaperman to lawmen, all of whom turned curious, impersonal eyes upon him, 'I cut hay all morning and raked it around the pond before lunch and this afternoon I was baling and planned on baling until dark but the baler wasn't picking up just right. It'd kick out a forty pounder and then a hunnert pounder, and then the threader broke down and the danged machine was spittin' out loose bundles and not cleaning up the windrows and finally I give up and come to the house, tired as I could be, and I opened the back door and seen this burglar standing there'—— He pointed, realizing as the heads turned to look that he'd gotten a bum start, that they were impatient with his too many words, that they wanted it all in a sentence, explained away. But he'd wanted them to see it just as he had seen it in the blue fall light, wanted them to understand his weariness and delight, his fear and his sudden sorrow.

Hemingway looked at the burglar still sitting there

67

against the pipes, his head at an uncomfortable angle, the blue eye and the red eye staring back at them, and said, 'It looks like he was especially made up for this type of an evening.'

'Well, get on,' the sheriff said. 'How'd it happen?'

While Harold took a breath, preparing to speak, his wife shoved in ahead of him and, in a brief statement or two, told it all. Harold was not listening. He was thinking that this was the first time she'd spoken up for him, explained for him. And it was also the very time he could not appreciate it. His face turned warm and dry with the knowledge of his own ingratitude.

When she finished, the sheriff nodded and Hemingway's one long stride took him to Harold's .38 lying on the cabinet. He handed it to the sheriff and then knelt and picked up the burglar's gun from out of the limp and lifeless hand. He looked at it, holding it under the light, and grunted, 'German made.' But Harold felt the stir of satisfaction only faintly. He was beginning to realize some vague premonition.

Hemingway clicked the burglar's gun open and shook it against his palm. He looked at Harold and then at the sheriff and he said one word, 'Empty!' Harold felt a sinking sensation in his stomach as they turned to look at him.

'This gun is empty,' Hemingway repeated. 'You kilt a man had an empty gun.' And for an instant Harold was afraid the patrolman was going to laugh.

Automobile lights swept across the window and

brakes squeaked as a third vehicle stopped in the yard and joined its headlight beams to the other two pairs remaining on out there, illuminating the geraniums. The sheriff shrugged. 'That'll be Javits.' Javits was the coroner and undertaker and funeral-parlor operator in Grand Junction. And before Harold had time to come out of his state, they swarmed for a moment around the kitchen and then they were gone, taking the dead man with them.

It seemed cruel to Harold that the gun was empty. And how was he supposed to have known? His wife said it was a clear case and that was all there was to it. In bed that night, Harold went over it all time after time from beginning to end until he had it firmly fixed—the mask, the black felt hat, the winter suit of clothes ('It looks like he was especially made up for this type of an evening'), the foreign-made gun, the words 'This is it!' The burglar was obviously The Burglar, as anyone could plainly see. And when he finally slept, he dreamed about the inquest. He'd never been to an inquest, and in his mind he confused it with a courtroom trial complete with a poker-faced jury, a black-robed judge, and a very suave lawyer who looked like Melvyn Douglas. And he, Harold Widkins, was on trial for his life. The decision turned on one point. He produced detail after detail—hat, suit, gun, mask—all marked on tags as Exhibits A, B, C, D. But he seemed unable to convince them that The Burglar was indeed The

Burglar. The courtroom grew tense. The judge was ready to lower his gavel with a pound. Then Mildred burst loose from the officer holding her back, ran weeping to fall at Harold's knees where he sat in the witness box, and said, 'Bring in the corpse and look. You'll find—' pause—'you'll find that, on his right hand, the tip of his index finger is missing.'

'I tried to keep my wife out of this,' Harold said in a voice with a manly ring to it.

But it was over. He'd won. Everybody crowded in to shake his hand and pound him on the back. And Melvyn Douglas, his face black with anger, muttered something that Harold thought must have been, 'I'll get you for this if it's the last thing I do.'

He was feeling gravely important, dressed in his blue serge suit with a white shirt and black tie, as he drove himself into town to go to the inquest. He tried to imagine his picture with the story in the newspaper, and the headlines—Hal Widkins Vanquishes Desperado. He liked to think of himself as Hal instead of Harold, but it was seldom any more that he could manage it, though when he was a boy in school he had signed all papers that way—Hal Widkins—with as much of a flourish as he could manage in his naturally crimped hand. The teacher, handing papers back, usually paused and squinted at the name and then said, 'Oh, Harold,' leaving him somehow mortified.

The inquest was a disappointment. It was held in

a small office on the balcony floor of the courthouse, where they all sat bunched in a circle on folding chairs. Harold never got it quite straight in his mind just what was the function of each of those in attendance. He wasn't given much of a chance to talk, and it seemed that most of what was necessary had already been written down. The man in charge said it was a simple case.

The Burglar had been identified. His name was Vernon Smith, and the name, taking the place of Burglar, came as a shock to Harold. Not only did the dead man now have a name, he also had an address. It was in a town not fifty miles away, a town by the name of Rapids City up on the river. And he was being taken back home on the afternoon train for burial. This stranger, Vernon Smith, also had relations, and they'd been notified and were expected at any time.

All that seemed to be left for Harold to do was to look once more at the body and to sign something. He followed the sheriff across the street to the morgue where they took him to a cool back room and showed him a body lying on a table.

Harold walked up to it and looked down. The face, without the mask, looked familiar to him. It must have been, he thought, that it looked like so many other faces—round and ruddy, with a mouth that seemed to be bruised. He did not remember that mouth. And the hair that he had not seen before was limp and fine, light brown and with a cowlick over the

71

forehead. The rakish sideburns had been shaved off and nowhere did Harold see the black felt hat.

'That's him,' Harold said, but it came out more as a question.

'Well?' the sheriff said, just a little bit impatient.

So Harold looked again. And now he saw that the body was no longer wearing the dark winter suit of clothes, but blue serge such as farmers wear on Sunday, such as Harold at this moment had on.

He swallowed. Nothing about this corpse lying with a certain decorum on the table identified him as The Burglar, and the smell in the room was making Harold a little bit sick at his stomach.

'They done a good job on the wound,' the sheriff said, and, grateful, Harold bent to look. But the patch on the right cheek looked as if it might have been put on with make-up. Then he remembered something. He looked at the hands, crossed there over the chest. The left hand covered the right one, and Harold had to lift it off in order to see what he was looking for. The feel of it, cold and stiff as the hand of a wooden image, further confused him and he almost forgot what he was after. He felt the sheriff's eyes upon him, curious. 'There!' he said, pointing to the index finger with its tip missing. The sheriff looked and grunted.

Harold straightened up and reached for the paper in the sheriff's hand. The sheriff handed it to him and obligingly turned his back for him to write against. Harold felt a wave of gratitude. Then the sheriff shook his hand and went out, leaving him done with and alone.

It was wrong. All of it, wrong. It was not as it should be. But as Harold turned to leave, he could no longer have said how it should have been. He only knew that he was unsatisfied, and empty, and confused, as if he'd heard a song go off-key or had a tube go out in the final reel and was never to know the ending, or listened to the greatest joke of his life only to have the teller forget the punch line so that he could not laugh. And this expectation—of tears or laughter or knowledge like a burst of light— built to a force inside him that now might never be released, like a mighty bubble of gas pushing fatally against his heart.

He did not at once see the people waiting for him to step aside so that they could enter. The sight of the man and woman dressed in their best for some occasion gradually focused out of the blur the world had come to be. They nodded, timid and unsure of themselves, and he returned their nods. The sheriff was out of sight and the undertaker, who'd brought them to the door, now turned his back and walked sedately back toward the front of his establishment.

The man glanced around and, when his eyes lighted on the table with its burden, he looked quickly back to Harold. The woman, her face swollen looking under its self-contained round hat, walked past Harold without looking at him again. But the man stayed

73

in the door and put out his hand. 'Smith. Vernon Smith,' he said.

Harold felt as if he'd like to run, but he could not move. He remembered the sensation from a certain recurring dream he'd had as a child. Fighting the impulse to hide his hand behind his back, he reached out and shook the proffered hand. But though he opened his mouth, he could not seem to think of his name. Behind him he heard a sob break from the woman like a gasp of fright.

Vernon Smith Senior was a pink-faced man with watery eyes that looked as if he were perpetually prepared to weep. 'He wasn't quite right,' he said. 'The boy never was quite right. A mule give him a lick in the head when he was a youngun.' He glanced toward his wife and lowered his voice. 'It wasn't that he was born thataway. There never was any—any kind of a taint in the family.' He looked at the floor, cleared his throat, and brought his eyes up. The watery blue eyes jerked over Harold's face with the persistence of water bugs moving on the face of a pond. 'His mother doted on him, though. Grieved over him. She always grieved over him.'

He made no move to cross the room to look at his son, but seemed rather like a man waiting for a woman to finish with womanish things.

'A woman,' he said, his eyes darting to Harold's mouth, forehead, chest, 'a woman don't accept things.'

Harold found himself nodding.

74

'I kilt the mule,' Mr. Smith said.

Harold nodded again, waiting. But that seemed to be all, the whole of it, and the man, seeing Harold wait for more, looked to oblige him.

'Are you the law?' he asked.

Fear and uncertainty gripped Harold in the intestines, and when they let go he felt that he had to hurry and find a men's room.

The man looked puzzled when Harold didn't answer. 'He was a good boy,' he said. 'Never give us no trouble till now. No taint in the family. At heart he was as good a boy as you would hope to find. Simple, that's all. Just simple.' Then he added, 'He was named after me,' in a voice that implied 'The best of everything' and 'Every opportunity under the circumstances.' He cleared his throat as if the gurgle were an old habit, as though something were stuck there that he'd given up hope of ever being rid of.

It was not until Harold was repulsed that he could fully recognize this man who stood before him as a man certain of his innocence stands before justice.

'I'm sorry as I can be,' Harold said.

The man nodded, accepting this as only right and due.

'You shouldn't have bothered,' Mr. Smith said, 'if it was hard for you to get away this morning.'

'It wasn't nothing,' Harold said, glancing quickly around the room to see if there might be another exit. But when his eyes came to the woman doubled up with grief beside the table, he turned back to the man barring his way.

'I known he had that gun,' Mr. Smith said. 'But I never thought he'd get into trouble with it long's he had no bullets.'

Harold said, 'Excuse me,' and tried to move around Mr. Smith, but his words were not clear and the man did not make room for him to pass.

'He tried to join the army,' Mr. Smith said, and Harold, for one awful moment, thought the man might be going to smile, or might be expecting *him* to smile. When Harold simply stood staring at him, Mr. Smith continued, 'He was always dressing himself up one way or another, but I never dreamed it would get him into any trouble. I known there wasn't a place for him anywheres in this life, but I tried to make him keep his eye on the hereafter.' His eyes shifted across Harold's face. 'I give a lot of my time to the church,' he said. 'I make calls every Sunday morning and pass the word along, for us that has it's got no right to hoard it to ourselves.'

'Are you a preacher?' Harold choked the words out.

Mr. Smith shook his head. 'I myself am not. But any questions you might have, I can get an answer to. And every answer comes smack from the Bible, the Word of God. Listen, if you ain't yet saved, there's not a whole lot of time.' He leaned toward Harold, lowering his voice. 'Read Revelations. It tells you right there.' He pointed a finger at his open palm as though his text might be transcribed upon it. 'Armageddon is upon us! "There shall be wars and pestilence." Now I don't have to tell you nothing about wars, for you know for yourself as well's I do there's been more wars in our lifetime than you could shake a stick at. And pestilence! Listen, do you keep a garden?'

Harold said his wife kept a garden.

'Have you ever before had more pests to cope with than you had this year?'

Harold agreed there'd been a plague of them.

Mr. Smith straightened up and crossed his arms, satisfied he'd made his point. 'Well, there you have it.'

Harold waited, not at all sure of what he had. But Mr. Smith had finished, was gazing across Harold's shoulder at the body of his son. His eyes swam, and Harold thought that now he would break down and his sympathy began to rise.

Mr. Smith said, 'I give a lot of my time to the church, and I give to the poor, and I believe I'm saved.'

Harold knew he had to get out, escape to some place where he could be by himself. He touched Vernon Smith's elbow and moved him aside.

'Pleased to have met you,' Mr. Smith said. But Harold was stumbling through the curtained door, hurrying away.

Alone in the street, he stood a minute to get his bearings, lost in this town he'd grown up in. He spent some minutes studying the clock on the front of the courthouse facing out over the square, but he didn't read the time.

Then he walked to the café across the street, though he was not hungry, and entered the long, narrow room lined on one side by dark old-fashioned booths and on the other by a modern chrome-lined counter and bright plastic-covered stools. He took a seat in the first booth he came to. The place was empty except for a tall hump-shouldered waitress reading a copy of *Silver Screen*. Someone had left a coffee-stained morning paper lying on the table, and his own face stared up at him, unshaven and surprised. The picture cut him off just across the chest, and the galusses of his overalls showed.

It was a shock to see himself lying there defenseless on the table, obviously unprepared. He gave the paper a shove, and it slid off onto the seat opposite him.

The waitress came with her pad and pencil, and when he said, 'Coffee,' she sniffed, pushed an end of hair back behind her ear, and went away without writing anything.

While he waited for the coffee, he couldn't keep from stretching his neck a little to see the paper. It was cupped against the back of the booth, and his face, somewhat distorted by the bend, looked back at him across the table.

He stared at the face. It was the face of a stranger. He felt that it was the way he had looked, but would never look again, as if the self that he'd been were now gone out of him, had been transferred to the image on the thin sheet of paper to stare back accusingly at the strange self across the table. He thought of his name, and it seemed to him to be the name of someone he had once known, a long time ago. He recognized after a time his feeling. It was the feeling he'd had as a boy coming out of a Tom Mix picture, as the horse shrank and disappeared, the gun became a toy, the chaps fell off him and the spurs lay on the street, limp twists of dirtied foil, and he was alone in the late afternoon, in the dying light, weak after the bright night of the Picture Palace, alone on an earth contrary, in a world he did not want to know. He saw that Harold had been a fool and Hal but an illusion, and preparing to rise and quit the booth, he took out his purse, opened it, and read the identification—White, Male, Age 52, brown hair, blue eyes, 5′ 9″ tall, weight 160 lbs. He held the card closer, read it again, and carefully refolded the purse and placed it in the inside pocket of his coat, as if it might be precious. Then he put a dime on the table, took up his hat, and walked out.

The waitress, stopping so suddenly to see him go that the coffee slipped over the edge of the cup, was angered until she remembered she'd seen him come out of the funeral parlor. She drank the coffee herself, absent-mindedly, as she found her place again.

The sunlight seemed too bright to Harold that August day, both blinding and illuminating. On top of the First National Bank a twenty-foot signboard urged him to INSURE THE FUTURE FOR YOUR LOVED ONES,

REST IN PEACE THAT THEY WILL KNOW NO WANT. THE FUTURE NEED NOT BE UNKNOWN, FOR CENTS A DAY ... And in front of the First Baptist Church the board advertised CHRISTIAN FELLOWSHIP EACH FRIDAY NIGHT AT EIGHT. The drugstore window held the remedy for every ill. But Harold was not reassured.

He turned slowly in the empty square, a lone man, stranger to himself, in suit and vest prescribed, yet naked in the light of this high noon, naked but for the weight that he now felt, heavier than any burden he had known. For previous burdens had all been personal, hence small, like the flu when there is not an epidemic. Now he felt that he was victim of a plague that raged the streets, invisible to all but him. And he must spread the word against it. What was it? What word would he say? To whom would he say it? For once in his life, Harold had no word at his command. But he felt that he must find Mr. Smith.

He stumbled like a man in heat stroke to the funeral parlor and found it now deserted. The curtain hung down, unstirred, between himself and that back room. He went toward it, laid hands on it, and drew it aside. The body was gone, the table bare.

'He's gone. He's not here.' It was the voice of Javits, the undertaker, behind him. Harold turned, without seeing the man, and went out again. From the station at the end of the street, the train bell tolled for the crossing. He came into the sun in time to see the long cars moving slowly out. And Vernon

Smith, struck once by the mule and once by him, was going home. 'I kilt the mule,' Vernon Smith Senior said again to him. And what was it he had wanted to say to Vernon Smith, Junior or Senior, too late? 'I kilt us both and now the two of us are dead and I don't know whether to be glad or sorry. We're in this together, Vernon Smith.'

He felt that he'd been blinded that he might see, crippled that he might walk, had killed and died that he might be born, become a fool in order to learn to trust his wisdom. He didn't know yet what he was— a giant among giants or a pygmy among pygmies. But at least he felt he was onto it at last, had it in his reach. And as he watched the train disappear, he hoped that the kick of the mule and the kick of the .38 had equaled out for Vernon Smith and that now he was no longer not quite right but right again at last, devoid of gun and mask and winter suit of clothes, in no more need of defense, taint of the father gone, joke told, life spent, and innocence recaptured.

There in the direct light of the sun, in the center of Grand Junction's namesake corner, Harold Widkins took off his hat and pledged himself to something as yet unknown.

THE MOURNER

THE tracks coming into Galleton wind down
the mountain walls that hold the valley in
a giant vortex, the town at its center. Once
on the valley floor, the skein is lost in a web of swirling
bands and innumerable junctions that converge, at
last, upon the yard and then the shed, a great steel-
ribbed maw, hollow, echoing, a skin-covered skeleton
without muscle or viscera, no heart, and an empty
womb.

Gabriel sat with his cheek against the train window,
one foot on his suitcase. It was dusk and the lights
outside were coming on. When the conductor
opened the door, the smell of the diner in the car
ahead sweetened the conditioned air. His stomach
muscles grabbed, sore and knotted from motion
sickness in spite of the bitter pills he'd swallowed. He
turned his face to the window and saw his reflection,
saw it and through it to vague moving masses and
figures in the yard. His face in the window was a
smear of black eyebrows unbroken over his nose,

and a long oval jaw and cheekline that might have hung from hoops on his ears like false whiskers, an easy face to caricature. The noise of the clacking wheels thundered for an instant before the conductor closed the door. The little boy across the aisle got up again for water. He'd kept on his hat all the way down from St. Louis, an imitation pith helmet, straw painted white, with Lion Tamer stenciled across the crown.

The other passengers began to stir, to stand and stretch and reach down luggage from the overhead racks. One old woman got her bundles together and trudged up the aisle to stand at the door. Then the aisle filled before the train stopped. He watched the boy's helmet topple as, outside, his father lifted him. He'd traveled alone, the lion tamer, now he was home again, a child. His face pouted and posed. Gabriel waited for the car to empty before rising and gathering his things.

A porter came toward him when he stepped down onto the platform. He shook his head and muttered, following the stragglers down the concrete stair and into the dank tunnel that led under the tracks to the terminal. He climbed the ramp. The station was bright after the tunnel and the train. The people, the booths, the benches like pews in a church were small under the domed ceiling three or four lost stories high. On the street outside, he set his suitcase down and waited for a taxi. Before him the long avenue pointed toward the heart of the city. Across

83

the mouth of the viaduct that spanned the railroad yard the neon sign bubbled—GALLETON, THE MAGIC CITY. And in smaller lights, HOME OF DIXIE STEEL. Beyond, the downtown lights blinked like afflicted eyes. Stars sparked the surrounding hills. Atop Bald Mountain the Iron Man held his torch. And away off across the valley the glow from the furnaces scorched the sky.

He hailed a cruising cab, climbed in, and gave the address. The driver grunted, reached back and slammed the door. 'First time in Galleton, son?'

The muscles of his stomach braced as the cab lurched forward. 'No.'

The cab entered downtown traffic. The tires caught the streetcar tracks, hummed a moment, and jumped aside. What's his hurry? Gabriel wondered. It used to take half an hour. A half hour. He wanted to sleep. Last night at this time . . . let's see . . . the night before, Salt Lake City. Last week . . . He backed away. He saw himself, a figure grown pin-size in distance. When he was a kid on his way to the dentist he'd thought, a half hour from now I'll be through it, tomorrow at this time . . . Or confession. It was the same when the nuns herded him with the rest across the schoolyard to the church, to confession.

They were through the city. The cab took all the shortcuts. He thought: for once, an honest cabby, prides himself on his honesty, a simple measure of worth, a matter of short cuts.

84

He watched the signboards and drugstores. The laundry: WE WASH EVERYTHING BUT THE KIDS. The parts shop with its yard of wrecks. We salvage everything but the . . . He let it go. There was the motel like an Indian village. Teepeetown. Heap big deal. He leaned forward and began to direct the driver. They were getting close now. In the fairgrounds the stock-car races were on. Gutted mufflers roared, rubber screamed. The circle of track was hidden behind a white board fence. Floodlights looked down on the race he couldn't see. The speakers blared, 'Round and round they go, where they stop . . .'

The cab turned off the avenue and climbed the hill. Now it crawled. Gabriel watched the houses pass. Now he could call the names of the people who lived in them—Mancini, Amendola, Vlato, Morello. And under the noise of the speedway, voices called across the street. It was good dark now, and behind the hilltop the blare of the furnaces sat like a sunburst on the head of a saint.

'It's up there,' he said.

The house was lighted from top to bottom, but there weren't any cars out front. When they stopped, he paid the driver and then stood looking up at the house while the cab drove off.

All there but the lightning rods and porcelain baubles. All there—turrets, bay windows, the round towers and coconut frosting. As real as Disneyland. Up they moved, Morello—Giardini—Vlato—Virciglio, up from the banks of the mill to the iced and frosted summit of the hill, out at last from the shadow of the railroad sheds, away from the giant furnaces, they moved. And with them, moving also into the many-storied ghosts of a dead time, the keepers of homes for the aged, and the Greek morticians.

The skinny figure of a woman tripped toward him down the sidewalk. He recognized her. Mrs. Ricardi. The name played in his head. Mrs. Ricardi. *Misericordia.*

He turned. *Misericordiam tuam. Miserere nobis.* Before she could recognize him, he climbed the bank and started up the path in the shadow of the trees. *In nomine Patris, et Filii* . . . He mounted the steps and crossed the porch and stood a moment looking through the screen door into the lighted hall before he pressed the bell. And whoever said you can't go home again? Home is where the heart is, cold and pickled in a bottle like the embryo of a freak. Home is where you hang yourself. Home sweet *homo sapiens*, conglomerate polygot *in nomine* . . .

The chimes of the doorbell sounded. *Sanctus, sanctus, sanctus*, blessed is he who comes . . .

A priest came toward him down the hall. His brother.

'Gabriel!'

'Hello, Vincent.'

'Thank God you've come. The funeral should have been yesterday, but Mamma wouldn't hear—not till you'd come. I didn't think—— If you wired, we didn't get it.'

'Where is she?'

'At the undertaker's. They'll be back soon. People keep coming.'

Gabriel set his suitcase down in the hall and walked into the living room. It was smaller and the wainscoting darker than he'd remembered. Vincent came behind him and took up his pipe from the smoking stand.

'I gave him the last sacrament myself,' he said.

Gabriel nodded.

'He lived a long life, and—' there was a shrug in his voice—'a good one.'

Gabriel turned and looked at him.

'A good life as he saw it,' Vincent said.

Gabriel yawned. 'Anything to eat?'

Vincent led the way back to the kitchen. The round oak table was laden with dishes that made a mountainous landscape under the white cover cloth. Gabriel lifted a corner and drew out a chicken leg. Vincent poured milk from a flowered pitcher and handed it to him.

Leaning against the door, he looked at the room while he ate. The linoleum was bright and new, but the naked light bulb hung yet from its knotted cord. He stripped off the last meat from the drumstick and washed it down with milk.

'What now, Vince?' he asked.

Vincent shrugged. 'They haven't much. The house —a little insurance.'

'Teena has a job.'

87

'She doesn't make a lot. This is a big house, expensive to keep.'

'They'll have to get rid of it,' Gabriel said. They looked at each other.

Vincent shrugged. 'Time enough to talk about all that later.'

Gabriel felt the nausea from the train returning. 'I'm all in,' he said.

'They won't be long now.'

He wandered through the rooms, Vincent strolling behind him, his hands in his pockets, his face behind its chimney of pipe smoke. He looked into the doorway of the dining room that had for years been his grandfather's bedroom. The old man had feared the stairs. He'd hoarded life, that old man who'd talked so much of heaven. Well, he was gone now. The bed was made. Not a crease or rumple marked where he'd been. Gabriel looked over his shoulder at his brother. 'A good life,' he snorted.

'Why don't you lie down?' Vincent said. 'I'll call you when they come. Go on, you look worn out.'

Gabriel went into the room and dropped across the bed. The light from the hall silhouetted Vincent in the door.

'Two kinds of people, Vince,' Gabriel said. 'Parasites and hosts.'

'Only one host, Gaby. One host for all of us.'

Gabriel grunted. 'Don't talk shop to me, Vince.'

'All right. Two kinds of people. So if you're not a host, then you're a parasite.'

'They teach you logic in the seminary, Vince?'

'Logic and ethics,' Vincent said. 'Be good to Mamma, Gaby. She's been beside herself.'

'Go away. Let me sleep.' He rolled on his side and waited to hear Vincent's footsteps down the hall before he closed his eyes.

The smell of the old man was in the room. It was in the pillows and mattress, the smell of stale tobacco and that sour smell common to old men and babies. Gabriel fell asleep. He dreamed of the forbidden cave he and Vincent had explored as children. The entrance was like a big groundhog's burrow, a hole under the hillside too steep for houses, where a little wood still grew. The place was called McFarland's Spring because at the foot of the hill, in the McFarlands' vacant lot, springs bubbled out of the ground, almost hidden by fern and lined with the soft limestone called soapstone. You could rub the smooth surfaces with wet hands and stir up a gritty lather.

To enter the cave, you had to slide on the seat of your pants. The hard-packed earth was always slick and moist. At the bottom you crawled under a rock and came out into a little room where the floor was always muddy. It was dark and dank, smelling of urine, for tramps used the place. There, they always whispered.

The bed sagged and Gabriel struck out, grasping for balance at the covers. He opened his eyes. His mother sat beside him, and for an instant he felt the old fear, the guilt, of being discovered with muddy trousers.

'Mamma,' he whispered. 'Mamma *mia*—'

She put her hand on his forehead, brushing back his hair. 'My Gabriello, my boy.'

Her eyes were a little wild, and her black hair stood high and wild on her forehead. She whispered wordlessly, her hands touching him as they might feel a child for broken bones.

He put his arms around her and tried to rise, but she fell over him, sobbing. He could see the glow of Vincent's pipe in the dim room and the picture of Vincent the child came tunneling back to him, Vincent out of the light, Vincent watching with hunger in his eyes while his hands found something to occupy themselves, a piece of string, a rubber band, something to twist while he watched there from the darkness the two of them together in the light. Gabriel let his breath escape slowly, forced out of him by the weight of her on his chest. When it was gone, he couldn't breathe again. He put his arms around her and raised up.

'How are you, Mamma? All right?'

'My boy—my Gahbee.'

Then Vincent switched on the light. Gabriel stood up, drawing her to her feet.

'Come in the parlor, Gahbee,' she said, taking his hand and leading him. 'Teena! Tony! Eva Marie! Your brother he's home. Come look at him.'

In the parlor she stood him under the light, holding on to his arm. 'Why you're so pale, Gahbee? You don't drink! You wouldn't do that to me.'

'I had a beard, Mamma. I shaved it off.'

'Oh, no beard, Gahbee. Let it show, your face. Why you hide your face?'

He led her to the big square couch with a walnut slatted back and eased her down. She caught his hand and he stood awkwardly before her.

'Gaby!'

He turned. His sister, Eva Marie, rolled toward him, looking, in her pregnancy, like a pyramid of bright-colored balloons. He stared at her. She'd been slim and beautiful when he saw her last, this gross woman. She hugged and kissed him, and he felt like a pole in her arms. Her husband Antony came behind her.

'Hallo, Gabriello. Long time no see. Your sister, she eat me outa house and home. Some woman. Whatta woman.' He shook his head at the wonder of her and pinched her bottom proudly. He was a small man, a grocer and keeper of fancy fruits.

They shook hands. 'Hello, Tony.'

'You oughta see our boys, Gabriello. We got big boys—like their mamma. Whatta girl!'

'Our last one, our Vincent, he's mean as you were, Gaby.' She giggled and shook. 'We wanted you to be Godpoppa to him.'

'Leavim alone, leavim alone. Tellim all that later,' his mother said.

Then he saw his aunt Teena standing in the door, miffed at having been so long overlooked.

'Have you eaten, Gabriello?' She'd show them who held this house together.

He nodded. 'Yes, Teena. How are you?' He bent

and kissed her lips, which she compressed tightly to hold her lipstick intact.

'Where's your bag? Your things oughta be got out and hung up. All the company we had, you'll need your clothes. I'll hang the wrinkles out.' She was a tiny thing, getting dumpy now, and she wore her skirts short to show off her little feet, of which she was very proud.

'It's too late, Teena. They've been too long in the suitcase.'

'You never know,' she said. 'Let me at 'em, no telling what I might do.' She winked. 'Save you a pressing bill.' She had seen his suitcase and now she went to pick it up. He moved to take it from her, but his mother grabbed his sleeve.

'Is she your mamma? Who's your mamma? Come here, sit by me.'

Teena struggled off with the weight of his canvas bag, mincing in her little shoes. He let himself be pulled down. They all settled in the circle of chairs that made the room look as if it were arranged for a meeting of some kind.

His mother put her hand over his, plucked his fingers, traced his knuckles, patted. 'Poppa's gone now, Gahbee.'

'I'm sorry, Mamma.'

'Are you, my boy? Yes, we must all of us grieve. He was such a strong man. Never did he miss a day's work in his life, Gahbee. Think of it! Not a day. We can all be thankful for that. He had his health to the end.'

Teena called from the kitchen where she'd hauled out the ironing board. 'A fine constitution. All the doctors said it, Gabriello. A constitution unheard of in a man his age.'

'And Gahbee's like him. They were like as two peas. That's why,' his mother nodded, 'that's why they never got on together. Too much alike.' She leaned toward him with her wild eyes. 'He said, Gabriel, Poppa said every day, "Tell that boy to come home where he belongs. Get him back here. If he's so set on painting, let him paint houses, all the houses on this hill. There's good money in that." ' She laughed. 'He'd be tickled to know he was the one brought you back, Gahbee. He was always one to have his way.'

'Fine figure of a man till the day he died,' Teena called in. 'And he laid out beautiful too.'

His mother was plucking his fingers again. 'Like as two peas. I tell 'em all. Gahbee's the one like his Grampa. All my children handsome and beautiful. But Gahbee's the one. Now Vincent, he's a fine fellow. But a priest got no business to be handsome. It's more against him. Turns the girls' heads and makes their mammas sick in church at the loss.' She laughed. Gabriel looked across the room at Vincent grinning in the doorway.

'Tell me where you live out there, Gahbee.'

'You got a car?' Tony wanted to know.

'I live upstairs at this lady's house, Mamma, like I wrote you.'

'Ahah!' Tony said. 'A lady!'

93

'How she feed, that lady?'

'She doesn't feed me. I just room there. I eat out.'

'At's no good, eat out! A growing boy needsa be fed at home.'

'Mamma,' he laughed. 'I quit growing.'

'Hah! Vincent, he grows still.'

Tony clapped his knee. 'In the belly.'

Gabriel looked again at Vincent, but he could not see his face clearly behind the smokescreen his pipe put out.

'Let *me* tell you about growing boys,' Eva Marie said, waving her hand. 'I got three and I know all about 'em. You only seen just the one, Gaby, my Andrew. The middle one, he's got them black brows with light hair, like you. Teena she says that hair, it comes from our father.'

Thump! His mother's fist came down on the walnut arm of the sofa. 'Don't speak of that tenor your father here in this house where Poppa passed. Oh, Poppa, he told me. But I wouldn't listen. Weak, he said, useless. More woman that one couldn't find nowhere than me, your mamma! Too much woman for that singer.' She laughed a short hoot of laughter. 'I give him children, fine children, all in a row. Vincent, Eva Marie, Gahbee. Beautiful children! And off he goes, Gahbee nothing but a child. And all my other children, them I never had . . .' Her shoulders shook, and her voice pierced. Gabriel felt somewhere deep under his ribs the long-forgotten but instantly familiar tremor, like the tremor set up in the house by the Frigidaire motor starting at night in the darkness under the cellar stairs, remembered from his childhood. Vincent crossed the room to sit beside her and take up both her hands.

'Mamma, now Mamma.' But she snatched her hands away from him.

'Let us pray, Vincent. Lead a prayer. The mysteries, the sorrowful mysteries, for Poppa.' She took Gabriel's hand and drew him closer. 'And the joyful ones too, Vincent, for my Gabriel come home.'

Antony heaved himself out of his chair and onto his knees. Gabriel heard the thud as Teena knelt beside the ironing board out in the kitchen. Vincent took out his rosary and helped his mother down. Only Eva Marie, solemn now in her pregnancy, tugged her skirts toward her knees and remained enthroned in the big wing chair. They waited. Gabriel plucked at the sofa cushion.

'On your knees,' his mother said. 'You will get down on your knees, Gabriello.'

He looked at her wild eyes, watched her hands grasp for him. The others did not look up.

'Kneel!' she shouted. 'You will this once be like us. Kneel to your God, Gabriello Orghesi. Kneel!'

Trembling suddenly to his scalp, Gabriel slid to his knees.

And quickly Vincent began.

Finally, in the car going to the undertaker's, Vincent asked him, 'You're going back?'

He didn't answer at once. He knew his brother's

mind. Why did you come at all? Then, angry at the words that, though unspoken, nevertheless lay palpable between them, he mouthed, 'The sooner the quicker,' and immediately despised his own facetiousness.

They rode in silence, Vincent too big for the car, a big dark giant whose hands on the wheel looked like a man's hands driving a child's push-pedal car. He hunched down to see out of the windshield.

Gabriel laid his head back and looked up at the sudden sun that leaped against the hill as steel was poured, like fire from a cauldron tipped in hell. And then came the roar. The city seemed then to him like a gigantic prostrate functioning body, pillowed on the hills. Eyes and arteries, now the bowels. The smell of sulfur seeped around the windows and rose up through the floorboards.

'God,' Gabriel said, 'I'd forgotten.'

The undertaker's establishment was the only building lighted now on the littered street. It was a one-story brick building that might have housed a grocery in this long-dying suburb under the plant, and it opened directly onto the sidewalk. No awning-covered walk, no tended grass, unnaturally green, no muted lights spotted on colonial false front, no euphemistic legend under glass like a church announcement of next Sunday's sermon attempted to call the place a 'funeral home'. It was simply, almost brutally, what it was, the undertaker's place of business. Inside, the walls, dirty from the mill, were watermarked in pale patterns, distortions by Dali. And against the smell of sulfur, no flower could have breathed. Lights blazed from naked ceiling hangings. Nothing here was indirect.

In the parlors old men lined against the walls, speaking in gruff whispers, a people consecrated to death, rededicating themselves each Sunday, and now in the middle of the week. It walked to meet them in familiar forms, diseased or crippled, seldom peaceful, and one had seen a brother drop from catwalk to cauldron of molten steel that blazed like an incandescent pool on the sun, had seen his brother drop and try to run across that viscous fire while his legs melted under him and, poised, startled on his shrinking stumps, he slowly sank, his mouth gaped open at whatever it was he contemplated. They lined the walls in awe, timid, speaking now and then in low tones the language that, like a wall, kept them isolated and safe in this world where their children walked away but where they would always stay, uneasy.

They stared respectfully at Vincent, the priest. They nodded when spoken to, suddenly bestirring themselves, pushing upright from the walls, smiling uncertainly, bobbing heads and twisting caps like wheels in their gnarled and scaly hands. And it would take a while for them to unwind and relax again against the walls. Gabriel felt their eyes on his back as he passed and they tried to place his familiar face.

He followed Vincent into the 'chapel' from which the body would be moved in the morning to the church. He tried to examine his feelings as he walked down the uncarpeted aisle where his footsteps clacked. He found no feelings to examine.

Vincent stepped aside into one of the pews to kneel, and Gabriel walked ahead. The body revealed itself to him in pieces, first the nose, unnaturally powdered, and then the shock of hair that had sprung loose from where they'd tried to paste it down. The unnatural darkness of the hair over that aged face, powdered and rouged, made the old man look strangely alive, like a young actor playing an aged corpse. And then he saw the fist and he thought: he died like that, clenching that fist, and they couldn't pry it loose. Someone had drawn a black rosary through the clamped fingers. The old man's hand gripped it like the collar of a thief he did not mean to get away. The rouge could not hide that burnt black mottling under the skin where the furnaces had left their brand. The fist, the mottled face, the springing hair would have mocked death had it not been for the undertaker's crude art that sought to make him 'natural.'

'I've come to bury you,' he said silently to the corpse.

The flared nostrils seemed to breathe and the stiff black hairs protruding seemed to quiver. Gabriel might have trembled like the boy he used to be had there not been the ludicrous art of the undertaker to reassure him.

He could hear the old man's voice shake with rage, scream, 'Not you. Death!' turning it to a privilege.

Hearing the voice, Gabriel felt the old man standing there at his elbow, looking critically down into the bright pink tufted box. He drew his shoulders in, shrugged, to rid himself of the phantom and to try to place the old man where he'd had him so he could speak without being interrupted. 'I forgive you,' he said. But again he heard from somewhere behind him, 'Who the devil do you think you are?'

He turned quickly and, without waiting for Vincent, went out past the pairs of shifting boots with high, creased tops and humped and rounded toes scarred by ends of pipe and corners of sheet and rails. A voice said '*Scuse.*' He waited on the sidewalk for Vincent to come out, and as they drove home again he closed his eyes, pretending sleep.

But he could not sleep, not even when, in his old bed, hard and narrow as the cot of a monk, he wrapped himself in darkness. He lay on his side and looked out the window and down across the street to where Mrs. Ricardi sat in her porch swing, silhouetted against the yellow light in her lace-curtained windows. How many nights had he gone to sleep watching her there? Mrs. Ricardi. The Wanderer. Living alone, spending her days over the neighborhood, from kitchen to kitchen, drumming her fingers, finishing sentences other people started——

'It's going to be——'
'A pretty day—a pretty day——'
'Fall——'

99

'Late—late this year—oh late——'

——impatient to be off again, Mrs. Ricardi. He knew he would see her there, if he woke early, waiting for signs of life, sipping her lemonade—for her bowels, she said, and she attributed to it not only her regularity, but her longevity as well. Then she would wander again, across yards, through gardens, down alleys, from house to house, her arms crossed and held tight to her flat slab of breast, her thin body driven by some wind that only she could feel. And eventually she would tell you how, when she was a girl, the sewing-machine people voted her Miss Twinkle Treadle and put her picture on their directions booklet and gave her a sewing machine free.

Across the valley he could see the television towers on the mountaintop. He thought of San Francisco, the lights on the hillsides, like luminous honey in a giant comb. Cassidy, Bowles and the others would be at the wharf now, cracking crab and drinking beer and talking. Cassidy would be doing most of the talking, the Right Reverend G. B. Shaw Cassidy. That big Irishman. 'You're a dreamer, Gabe,' he'd say. 'Me, I'm a realist.' And he drew a picture of the world exploding —all very detailed in the dismembered bodies and blood in the manner of a medieval rendering of hell, and in the corner a serene little figure with a beard painted children's blocks on a Mondrianesque canvas. 'That's you, Gabe,' Cassidy said.

'Take up writing, Cassidy,' he answered. 'You're good at anecdote.'

Composition, architecture—Cassidy said a painting must have those things. The painter's duty to mankind —and, more important, mankind's duty to the painter. The painter, in Cassidy's philosophy, deserved to be kept and coddled like a concubine. Modern art was irresponsible because it was 'Rarefied, escapist.' Cassidy liked words. But Cassidy was a realist. He painted things—tables and apples and chairs and cats.

In the beginning Gabriel had talked too. 'What is real?' he asked. 'You think this table—that cat—they are reality? They are things. Put them before you they become a wall. Things are walls to go through.'

'Then go through them,' Cassidy would shout. 'Don't for God's sake deny they are there.' And he would try to persuade him he must go to the University (where he could take classes from Cassidy). An artist cannot be illiterate, he would say.

And Gabriel would wave a blessing in the air before Cassidy's face, intoning 'Universitas Californiensis.'

Whereupon Cassidy, incensed, would grumble off, and he and Bowles would sit until the fish houses closed and then move up to Chinatown, and be caught by morning in a Settlement basement watching those strange young men and women who spoke a language more foreign than the Chinaman, who claimed the city as theirs and reduced art and God and the sidereal universe by the most common denominator, who loved their fellow man (so long as he was filthy, diseased, destitute, or mad), who sometimes turned on him and Bowles and said, 'Speak, man, speak.'

And sometimes Bowles would speak to them while they listened intently, 'Gone, man, gone.' And Gabriel would compose his face while Bowles reveled in nonsense to see how long they'd listen before recognizing it. Bowles had three degrees. He knew it all. But he only believed one thing—that there were no answers for Bowles. And, poor fellow, he was a good painter, better by far than Cassidy, good enough to know how mediocre good can be.

'Now you, Gabe, maybe you've got it.' He attributed it all to a Southern-Italian-Catholic background. 'You've got plenty driving you away. Maybe if they drive you far enough you'll get there. Maybe you'll do it, you're ignorant enough, you've never learned the horror of tolerance,' he would say toward morning when he was, mercifully, drunk at last.

It was only when he was very sleepy that he let himself think again of the old man lying ill at ease in death on the tufted pink in a dark and unfamiliar place, locked up, a commodity in a box, alone for this long night. He saw again the fist that had not meant to clutch a rosary. He asked, When did it come, this anger like a yoke we wore, binding us and holding us apart? I am my father's son, he said to the presence listening, angry, inarticulate. Whoever he was, that singer of Italian arias, I'm his, however bad you hated. For I saw early that simple truth in your fierce and vengeful eyes when you looked at me, at the brush in my hand, at the wobbling homemade easel, and asked if I didn't want to sing. He said, The anger came the day you cut my hair and, shorn and grim, I yet refused to bawl; it came when at the age of twelve I was by your commandment circumcised; it came when I, sixteen, crept in from being with a girl and you and your razor strop preached chastity and virtue. You're dead, he said to the presence, go lie down.

When he slept, he was riding again, across the luminous wastes of the salt flats at night, lost in that northern desert the color of leprous flesh. And over and over he dreamed those words he'd prayed as a boy here in this place from which he'd never hoped to escape: Oh God, grant me one grain of the salt of Thy wisdom—one grain—and I will carry the sacrament of it to the altar of my own fashioning on the peak of this earth where it may illumine mankind forever and ever, amen. Your servant, Gabriello Orghesi. And P. S. Oh my Father, deliver me.

In nomine Patris, et Filii. Before the altar, black-vestmented, the priest, his brother, raises hands. And in the aisle, the bier. *Oramus te, Domine*. Bows down to kiss the stone.

Credo in unum Deum . . . Suscipe . . . Pater Noster, qui es in coelis . . . Libera nos, Domine . . . Per omnia saecula saeculorum . . . Dominus vobiscum . . . Benedicat vos omnipotens Deus Pater et Filius, et Spiritus Sanctus . . . Deo gratias.

Through it, Gabriel sat, knelt, stood, the responses on his tongue, before the museum, the shrine, the tabernacle opening to gape. 'I forgive you,' he said. And the old man thundered.

Later, beside the open grave, he stood long after all the prayers and holy-water sprinkling. His mother plucked his arm. 'Gabriello, come.'

He pulled himself free and finally was left alone under the tent, hearing the caravan of cars, feeling the black-robed presence of Vincent up the green slope, waiting. The gravediggers, sullen at his interfering presence, began their tasks. Up came the rails, the canvas straps, away the paper grass. And there the earth—naked raw red gash exposed. He took up a shovel and onto the dull glow of the coffin the fresh dirt spattered. But while he leaned on the shovel and watched, the old man stood beside him, at his elbow, watching too. Defeated, he flung down the shovel and turned.

Vincent slid behind the wheel and there between them the old man sat.

At home he gathered up his things in the canvas bag and zipped the zipper while she wailed beside him and his stomach, knotting, felt like the stomach of a bilious child. Impatient, he waited in the kitchen while she packed a shoe-box lunch for him to take along, fussing Teena, miffed acolyte, out of her way. Hysteria sat like a mask on her face. Silent in the front room with lingering friends, Eva Marie and her frightened boys.

'I'll send you money every month,' he said, able to speak now it was so close. Later he could think of how.

'Money!' she cried.

He stood at the door of the old man's room, smelling the aged smell of him, seeing the imprint of a body on the spread.

He shivered, then remembered it was his own.

Then through the city again, two cars to the station. Himself and Vincent, their mother, *the old man*, in one. Behind them, Eva Marie and the boys in the furious chariot Teena hurled against the traffic, her little foot determined on the gas, her neck craned so she could see out at all.

On the noisy platform they huddled around him, all but Vincent, who held himself apart, puffing too vigorously upon the pipe in his clenched teeth. The boys shouted shrilly over exploding steam, listing what they wanted of the West. Horses. Guns. Real hats and leather chaps. A tumbleweed. One Indian (they were being reasonable). Some ropes.

His mother, gesturing with her hands, was suddenly quite gay. If she breaks, he prayed, let it be after. She told him to eat and say his prayers. He reached for the shoe box under her arm, but she turned aside.

'Anh-anh, not yet, Gabriello. I got a surprise.'

'She's going too!' one of the boys shrilled over the conductor's 'All aborrrt.'

Gabriel whirled, sought the faces that smiled their sly secret, all but the closed up face of Vincent behind his formidable pipe.

'That's right, Gabriello,' she said, hugging the shoe box, moving to the step a porter flung down below the high door of the coach. 'Why you think I pack so big a lunch, hah?'

He backed into the shadow of the train, facing them. But he knew it was a joke and he had to help them with it. He turned to laugh with her, but she was gone. He saw the shoe box disappear into the train, helped aboard by the conductor who looked at him and shouted again, 'All aborrrt!'

They piled upon him, the boys and Eva Marie, kissing, while Spartan Teena stood aside, a tableau of courage under fire. And Vincent took his pipe out of his mouth and stepped up to shake his hand and grasp his arm. Gabriel wrenched free.

'No. Look here, Vince, what's the meaning——'

But Vincent took his arm again. 'Hurry.'

'Vince, what's she doing, Vince! Vincent!'

But he was standing on the steps, hoisted up by his brother, who stood on the bottom step, barring his way. 'Go along with it,' Vincent hissed into his face.

'Get her off of here!'

'You can do this one thing.'

'No. Not with me. She can't go. Not with me.'

'You are a fool,' Vincent said, his face straining red while he clung there and the train began to move. The others waved and shouted. He glimpsed tears on Teena's face as the edge of the car cut off his view of her. The others, fat Eva Marie and the shouting boys, ran alongside. 'Jump, Vincent! Jump down!'

'You've tricked me,' Gabriel shouted into his brother's close face.

'No,' Vincent said. 'Tony will meet her just outside the valley. He's gone already to the junction.'

And then as the train lumbered out from under the shed, Vincent leaped back and ran for a moment alongside. Gabriel's last view of his face caught his smile and his stout contempt. He'd proven something to himself.

The conductor touched his arm and Gabriel let himself be hoisted to the coupling bridge. He made his way down the swaying aisle to where she sat, smug and for the moment happy, untying their lunch. He stopped an aproned boy and bought two bottles of pop and sat beside her.

'Is nice surprise, Gabriello?'

He forced a smile and nodded, seeing Vincent's face, *the old man.*

'Califorr-nyah!' She waved a sandwich. He caught her hand and took the sandwich from her.

'You eat better now I take care of you, Gahbee.'

He stuffed the sandwich in his mouth. The seat ahead was empty. He flipped the back and moved across to face her. She drank from her bottle and pressed against the window, looking out. Now the train began to climb. They entered a tunnel, and when they came back into the sun, her expression had changed. The sandwich was limp in her hand and the pop no longer fizzed. 'You don't look happy at my coming, Gabriel.'

'Mamma.' He reached across the space and patted her knee, seeing Vincent laughing from the shadows, Vincent the boy alone, disdaining their sandwiches.

'We have us a time, hah?' Now she laughed. 'We have us picnics out there?'

'Lots of picnics.'

'I can pose for a picture, Gahbee. Remember that time? You made you that—whatcha callit?'

'Easel.'

'Yes. And I sit down and let my dinner burn. Remember?'

'I remember.'

'And you call it Madonna. Is sacrilegious.' She laughed. 'You was just a boy.'

Then, recalling his infirmity, she took a pill from her large black pocketbook. 'Here, right this minute, swallow.'

He took the yellow pill on his tongue and washed it down while she followed the movement of his throat.

'You don't look like Poppa,' she said. 'You look like that singer.' And she lapsed back into silence, staring at the wall of clay outside and close to the window, passing in a blur, dizzying.

Five minutes more and they'd emerge upon the summit. Five minutes after that and Tony's face would grin up at them, pleased at his part in the conspiracy.

'We got us a long trip ahead,' she said sadly.

He laid his head back and gave in to weariness. He had accomplished it. He had returned and now he left again. *Libera nos, Domine. Gratia.* He heard her spring and felt her at his side.

'Sick already!'

He shook his head, feeling the surge of the curving

cars and her kneading fingers on his hands. She pulled his head to her shoulder and stroked his hair.

'Gabriello—Gahbee—my boy,' she crooned.

He allowed himself the pillow of her, for soon they would emerge from that steep place onto a plain and he would be alone. The clacking wheels turned and churned and birth is not a thing of ones, one spasm, one swelling, one hour of pain, one cry. Between the wombs of woman and the grave, upon this belly earth, the fetus re-enacts itself a thousand times; breath tears and struggles in its caul; the shroud awaits; the angel of despair spreads wings like nets to catch the risers; bear your birth, the angel said. He allowed them both this sleeping moment before the rent, the breaking tears, the cry, before this monster he was riding bore him off again to peace and loneliness.

HUMMERS IN THE LARKSPUR

HALF the female population of Chickasaw Cross sat fanning itself on Rosalee Atkins' front porch the morning the van backed up to the old Currer place next door. Behind the van, a black open-top car pulled to the curb, and two women and a child got out. One of the women, big-boned, with black hair pulled tight and done in a bun, went up the walk and into the bungalow right away. The small woman with pale feathery hair cropped short as a boy's stood beside the van while the men struggled with the thick rope that tied up the tail gate. And Rosalee Atkins wondered aloud why on earth they'd brought a furniture van when they'd rented the Currer place already furnished. The child walked inside the picket fence, dropped cross-legged on the grass, and touched lightly with her fingertips a dandelion fluff, her skirts up about her waist. Rosalee Atkins said she appeared to be six, and when *she* was six she knew enough to keep her dress down.

They all there on the porch nudged each other when Ullus Wingo rounded the corner and, after watching from across the street for a moment, ambled up to the blonde young woman. Mate Atkins slammed out the front door in his sock feet, scratching the fur on his chest, and bawled, 'Howdy do, ladies.' Rosalee shushed him and pointed.

The vanmen had untied the rope and were easing the tail gate to the ground. The women on the porch strained to see through the wisteria vine. But whatever was inside was wrapped in quilting and bound. They could see only that it was big.

Then, as the men climbed into the van, the blonde young woman must have felt Ullus Wingo pluck at her sleeve, for she turned. The women on the porch leaned forward. Mate Atkins' laugh wheezed out, a sound like a burst of steam.

And because Ullus Wingo's voice had the bell-like quality of a child's, they heard the greeting he'd been taught by his seamstress mother to use for all strangers. 'My name's Ullus Wingo and I am retarded.'

The woman looked at him a moment before she spoke in a voice so low some of the women immediately turned to the others, whispering, 'What? What's she say?' and were quickly hushed so the others could hear if she said more.

'How d'you do, Ullus Wingo. My name is Mrs. Sean.'

Rosalee turned to her husband Mate and said, 'There. What did I tell you?' For Mate, who'd once shipped aboard a freighter out of Galveston, had argued that if it was spelled S-e-a-n it must be pronounced like sea with an 'n' added. Seen. And the whole town had taken his word for it.

'Rhymed with "lawn," sounded like,' one lady said. Another repeated, 'Shawn,' and someone else hissed for quiet. They watched, stupefied, breath held, for the woman was giving her hand to Ullus Wingo, and he stared down at it, looked at her face, then reached to touch the hand, to feel it, and, as Rosalee Atkins recalled later, she *let* him.

Then the grunting, panting vanmen adjusted the massive bundle above the waiting dolly while the woman whirled, put out a cautioning hand, and said something the women on the porch didn't catch.

'A grand piano!' Rosalee Atkins said. 'Currer's upright don't suit them.'

Nathaly Tatum dabbed her lavender handkerchief to her lips. She'd kept her silence till now, telling herself they were all aware that if anyone knew anything at all about the strangers it was she, and if they didn't want her opinion she wasn't going to force it on them. 'Perhaps she plays,' she murmured. 'It'll be nice for the church if she does.'

'*If* she's a churchgoer,' Rosalee Atkins said.

At that they narrowed speculating eyes upon the blonde young woman as she backed up the walk, cautioning the men as they struggled.

'Listen at that,' someone remarked. 'Now where does talk like that come from?'

'I do believe it's foreign,' said Nathaly, who'd once been away to school.

'Ain't Dago,' Mate said.

Someone asked, 'If it's a piano, why doesn't it have any legs?' But no one answered. The men eased their burden through the french doors that opened onto the garden. Then the woman and the men and the piano disappeared inside.

Nathaly Tatum sighed. As the particular friend of Bertrice Currer, she was responsible for what information the ladies had on the strangers. Now, as she spoke, the women listened, though they gave no sign of moving their interest from the house next door. 'Bertrice said to me just before she left for Rodgersville that they'd only rented for the summer.' They'd heard this bit before and now paid it no mind. Nathaly continued, 'They must be summer people, like the coast gets in season. Maybe they looked at a map and couldn't tell we were a little out of the way. Chickasaw Cross is a very long name. I've seen maps where it extended right out into the Gulf.'

They gave no sign of having heard this either. Rosalee Atkins stuck out her chin, stretching her lower lip taut over her teeth, and plucked at chin hairs with her fingernails while she squinted out through the vines. Nathaly thought it a disgusting habit for a circle leader to have. Nathaly, who prided herself on her personal habits, her good taste, her breeding, thought it shameful the way some women let themselves go. Very likely, she thought, Rosalee Atkins, because she happened to live next door, would set herself up as some kind of authority on the strangers—she, a woman with no sense at all of the correctness of things, who'd never been away in her life, who could hardly be expected to have anything at all in common with a woman who played the piano and drove her own car.

The men were coming out of the house now, the woman behind them. Again they climbed into the van bed and were for a moment lost to the sight of the group on the Atkins verandah. The women waited in silence. They clearly heard the Sean woman call out, 'Gently. Gently, please.'

'Two pianos! Now what on earth would anybody want with two pianos?'

Mate Atkins, sitting on the top step in the sun, said, 'Maybe she plays with both hands.' And his laugh sprayed over the sleeping four-o'clocks.

'Look,' Rosalee whispered, pointing to the little boxed-in garden where the elfin child knelt in the uncut grass. Ullus Wingo was sitting cross-legged opposite her, plucking dandelion fluffs and holding them for her to blow.

The women looked at each other while out on the walk the men struggled with the second piano.

They were all there to watch them come, and, at the summer's end, they were there to see them go. Of what happened in between, any in Chickasaw Cross could tell.

Mrs. Sean, the small, baby-haired one, was not often seen out of her garden. The marketing was done by the big one, Miss Sean, whom the child was heard to call Dodo. And Ullus Wingo accompanied them each time they appeared, the market basket swinging on his arm.

Often in the morning the sound of piano music came from the house. But rarely was a piece finished. The music seemed to come in snatches, though, as Rosalee Atkins reported, you couldn't be sure it wasn't all one piece, strangest racket she'd ever heard. And it wouldn't last long. Before an hour was up, Mrs. Sean would leave the piano to walk out into the garden. She'd sit beneath the umbrella tree and watch the child play in the grass. And from his perch on step or fence post, Ullus Wingo also watched. The child seemed not to notice so many eyes (there were, of course, Rosalee Atkins' too) but would play her silent, twirling play as if she were alone.

One Sunday afternoon shortly after the arrival, Nathaly Tatum paid her social call. She was the first. Through the years, cunningly as a hummingbird builds its nest, Nathaly had devised a personality for herself. As a child she'd been most awed by those who had opinions ready-made and applicable, who could say promptly that they liked or disliked this or that. Then, at fifteen, the year she was away at boarding school, upon hearing a sophisticate remark that 'blue is my color,' she'd found the key. She began by taking forever unto herself lavender. Her dressmaker suits were piped with the color, her room papered in lavender iris upon an ivory background. She did not wrap herself in it, but used it subtly, as 'flavor,' she would have said. Then, less timid, she explored afield. She discarded all bottles from her dresser save the cologne called Opalescence.

And thus, by degrees, she acquired herself—*her* color, *her* scent, violets *her* flower, and even her voice and laugh. She was never more bothered by the wonder who am I, for she had but to sniff, to look, to listen, and be met by the comforting answers. Likewise, the voice of Chickasaw Cross told her who she was. 'Nathaly's a born organizer,' it said, or, 'Nathaly keeps up.' Above all it said, 'Nathaly's the last of the Tatums.' That did not nearly express it, but it was enough. For Nathaly, in her century-old raised cottage surrounded by the remains of formal gardens, was a town institution, like the Civil War cannon in the park, or the ancient live oak that naturalists from the State University came annually, with their classes, to wonder at. She considered it her duty—nay, her right —to call first upon the Seans.

Accordingly, on a Sunday afternoon she got all dressed up in a linen suit piped in lavender, with lavender shoes, purse, and gloves, and, scented lightly with Opalescence, she tapped at the door of the Currer house.

Dodo answered. Nathaly paid her call, but she paid it to Dodo alone. Mrs. Sean was said to be resting. Afterwards, try as she would, Nathaly couldn't make much to-do of the conversation that had ensued. She repeated that yes, they liked Chickasaw Cross, but no significant tones came of it. 'Very closemouthed,' she said. Then, remembering that Nathaly Tatum never said an unkind word about anybody, she added, 'It's only natural for foreigners to be a little shy.'

Though the conversation carried no innuendo, Nathaly aroused more interest by recounting in detail the changes wrought in Bertrice Currer's living room. The sofa had been kept, a little low mosaic table had been set in front of it, and there was the addition of a large phonograph. Besides these bits of furniture, the only other things in the room were the two grand pianos, one with its top and keyboard closed and a rug draped over it, the other open, the lamp on in the daytime, as if someone might at any minute be going to play.

Nathaly had commented to Dodo, 'Your pianos are very nice.' But since her only answer was a nod and 'Yes', she omitted that from the telling. She had several observations to make: (one) there was a picture of a dark man with the most *pene*trating eyes; (two) she couldn't think of another house in town with a living room that could accommodate two grand pianos; and (three) the phonograph had been on rather loud when she entered and Dodo hadn't turned it down, and she'd had the distinct feeling that it was going for some purpose. She said she'd commented that the music was nice—though it's more probable she'd pronounced it 'just lovely'—and Dodo's answer was, again, 'Yes.'

After that, three ladies called in a body. They too were entertained by Dodo, who made no reference to Mrs. Sean until asked point-blank, then said that she was resting. The child had been playing at the open piano when they entered, and they begged her to play a little something for them. She had by this time slid off the bench to stand watching them enter. But obligingly, without a trace of shyness, she climbed back onto the bench, played a piece, got down, and stood quietly while they made over her. They said she was a pretty little thing, she had a gift, and she ought to go on Major Bowes. One lady asked her what it was she'd played. She looked at the lady incredulously, glanced at Dodo, and said, 'Mozart, Wolfgang Amadeus.' Then she spelled it out for them. The ladies were delighted, but Dodo seemed displeased. She excused the child, who did a quick little half-curtsy and went upstairs.

It was then that there came a tapping at the french doors, and Ullus Wingo entered. When he saw the visitors, he stood still, clutching several worn copies of the *National Geographic* to his chest.

'Good evening, Ullus,' Dodo said. A grin surfaced on his mercurial face. 'There's milk in the jug and cake on the kitchen table. Go and help yourself. Katherine will be down when she leaves her mother.'

'You know,' one lady said when he had gone, 'he's not right—here,' and she tapped her temple. 'Never has been.'

'It's a caution the way he takes to children,' Rosalee Atkins said, 'and him going on thirty if he's a day.'

Dodo inclined her head. 'He keeps our Katherine entertained.'

'Well,' said Rosalee, 'there's little Tommy Hollis across and down the block. Cutest child, and just as smart!'

Then the little girl came back down the stairs, passed the visitors, and placed a record on the phonograph. She listened to the opening notes, turned the volume up, looked toward the stairs as if waiting to hear a voice. When it did not come, she excused herself and went out to the kitchen. Dodo did not readjust the volume, and very shortly after that the ladies left.

At the next meeting of the church circle, Nathaly Tatum brought up the idea of a music club. The ladies immediately saw the possibilities and agreed that Chickasaw Cross had long needed just such a society. They bemoaned the fact that Chickasaw Cross showed so little interest, for all their efforts, in the arts, and Nathaly said, 'Honestly, sometimes I do believe we live in a cultural desert.'

Once the motion was made and carried, Nathaly rose with a name for the society. 'I've been stricken with an inspiration,' she announced. The inspiration had come the night before during a movie short. 'Let's call it the Summer Musicale.' The ladies were overwhelmingly enthusiastic. (Later Mate Atkins wheezed out a laugh, clapped his thigh, and said it ought to be called the High C's.)

It was decided, also by unanimous vote, that it would be no more than neighborly to ask Mrs. Sean to be guest performer at the first meeting of the Musicale. Nathaly was duly appointed as a committee of one to proffer the invitation.

The very next afternoon Nathaly, again dressed in her lavender-piped suit, stopped by the public library en route to the Currer place in order to bone up on her music. She looked through the index and table of contents of a book on music history, was dismayed by the dust that whoofed out upon her lavender jabot, said, 'Oh, yes' when she recognized the name Bach, looked up a bust pictured on page 233, and put the book away.

When she came to the Currer house block, she saw Dodo leave the yard with the child and Ullus Wingo. She slowed her walk until they'd rounded the corner and disappeared. Mrs. Sean stood at the gate, watching the departure. As she turned back to the house, she was caught by Nathaly's call.

'Yoo-hoo, Mrs. Sean! I'm so glad I've caught you at home. I was so afraid—my, it is a warm day, isn't it. And yesterday too. I don't know when we've had a breeze. I do believe it's the hottest day we've had.'

Mrs. Sean unlatched the gate. 'Please come in. I'm just having tea.'

'Well, I say. You English and your tea. I *am* right? You *are* English?'

Mrs. Sean led her to the wrought-iron chairs and table that had appeared in the garden. They sat down.

'My husband was Irish, but I——'

'Oh, my dear,' Nathaly exclaimed, 'I *am* sorry—sorry, I mean, that he's passed on.'

Just then the door behind them slammed. Nathaly had to turn. For a moment, she was speechless. Then, 'Why, Louella!'

The Negro girl didn't answer. She walked barefoot across the grass, set the tea tray upon the table, and went back into the house.

'Why that's Louella!' Nathaly said.

Mrs. Sean nodded, smiling, as she took up the cup and saucer. 'Sugar?'

'Does she *work* here?'

Again Mrs. Sean nodded. 'Lemon?'

Nathaly could only take the cup of tea and set it down upon the table. 'Well, I declare. She's never worked before. She's certainly been a problem. How on earth did you do it?'

'Do—?'

'Get her to come to you, I mean.'

'But she simply appeared and asked. That was all.'

'Well, I say. She's been a problem here for years.'

'How a problem? Such a child!'

'She's fifteen if she's a day, and to my knowledge hasn't worked a day in all those fifteen years. She's got white blood, as you can tell. But we don't know to this day who—— Her mammy died bearing her, and the other one who knows isn't likely to let on. We've tried everything with that girl. She won't work—or never would before—and she won't take anything you try to give her. Just walks around in rags until she's positively indecent and then presents herself at some door. Hardly says a word, just stands there and waits until you give her a dress to cover herself. Once Arabelle Snow offered her four before she'd take one. Waited, I mean, till she saw one suited her fancy. Well, I declare. Came here, you say.'

Mrs. Sean sipped her tea. (Afterwards Nathaly told the ladies of the Musicale that her eyes were black as peas—something you'd never guess for that light-colored hair—and you couldn't see what was going on behind them.)

'Why, once I said to her, "Louella, I'll fix up that little house in my back yard for you. It won't be any trouble now I don't keep hens, and you can have it all to yourself. The work's light and I live alone. There's hardly any washing. Why, I could do it myself. And I only require that you take baths regularly." And she said to me, "Miss Nathaly, you know well's I do no amount of scrubbing can take the nigger smell." Then she laughed like a hyena and ran away.'

Nathaly looked hard at the face across the table, but there was only the smile over the tea cup. She saw that she'd got off on a subject that did not hold Mrs. Sean and, as Nathaly had all the social graces, she cast around for a different topic. Then she remembered her invitation.

'Well, depend on me,' she laughed. 'I almost forgot. I dropped in on you today as a delegation of one—her laughter trilled—'representing the Chickasaw Cross

Summer Musicale. We voted unanimously—and *that* doesn't happen often—to invite you to be our guest performer for our first concert of the season.' She waited for Mrs. Sean's polite protestations, but her hostess didn't speak. She hurried on. 'We don't dictate the programs. You could just suit yourself on that. All the members are *so* enthusiastic. I do hope you'll say yes. And, just for me—I wouldn't for the world have the others know I asked—would you play some Bach? He's my favorite.'

Mrs. Sean's dark brows knit together. Carefully she fitted her cup back into its saucer and said, 'You are very kind. But, my husband and I—we were—what do you say?—a team.' She gave the word two syllables. It took Nathaly a moment to reduce it again to one.

'Oh,' she said, 'I've always said that's the only way, if a marriage is to work, the only way.' She smiled her sympathy.

Mrs. Sean studied her guest, frowning, then shook her head. 'No-no. I mean I cannot perform alone.'

'Oh,' Nathaly said, 'I know just how you feel. But if Papa told me once he told me a thousand times, if you fall off a horse, you must climb right back up again. That was his way of putting it. But, oh, he thought it was the only thing. You couldn't ask for a more sympathetic audience than the Musicale members. I do hope you'll see your way to coming. Maybe you'd rather just lecture. That would suit us to a T.'

Mrs. Sean looked bewildered, as if her command of the language had broken down. Nathaly was about to try again when the gate creaked. She turned. Dodo and the child walked toward them, Dodo to stand beside Mrs. Sean's chair. The child went to the table, curtsied to Nathaly, and poured a cup of tea, which she then sat sipping.

'Why, Miss Sean! I'm so happy I didn't miss you altogether,' Nathaly said. It was a fib. She found the dark woman somehow intimidating. But she chattered on, making herself pleasant. 'I've just been issuing an invitation to Mrs. Sean to play for our group, the Chickasaw Cross Summer Musicale. We're delighted by the prospect. We've heard such tempting snatches from your windows.'

Dodo laid a hand on Mrs. Sean's shoulder. 'My sister-in-law is suffering the shock of her husband's recent death, Miss Tatum. And she is undertaking the grave and difficult task of preparing herself for solo concert engagements. She has a reputation to maintain here and abroad, a program to prepare. She cannot take on more just now. I must insist—' and now she directed herself to Mrs. Sean—'that she refuse.'

Nathaly was quiet as a mouse, watching. For the moment, she felt, had a current to it. The younger woman met Dodo's impelling eyes with determination and good humor. She laughed gently. 'Dodo would put me in a glass cabinet,' she said, turning back to Nathaly. 'It is my belief that people must not be set apart. That is true, don't you agree?'

But Nathaly felt this was getting somehow beyond the bounds of polite conversation. She didn't immediately answer, and Mrs. Sean said, 'I shall be happy to play for your group, Miss Tatum.'

'Oh,' Nathaly breathed, a bundle of nerves. 'That's lovely, just lovely of you.' She hurried to rise. 'I'll schedule you for a few words too, just some little introductory preface. Anything will do. Well, I really must be going. Tempus fugits so.' Her laughter climbed the scale.

As Nathaly backed away, Dodo moved, but Mrs. Sean's fingers alighted on her wrist. Later Nathaly recalled that she'd felt threatened by the woman, really and positively threatened.

Emiline Cartwright, the Methodist preacher's wife, offered the church auditorium for the concert. It had the one grand piano, besides the two at the Currer place, in Chickasaw Cross. The concert was held late on a Sunday afternoon, and for it all the ladies turned out in long dresses. Nathaly Tatum said to Mrs. Sean as she met the open car at the curb, 'I guess this sort of a to-do is new to you all. But we believe in dressing up for an occasion, and we certainly regard this as an occasion.' Katrine Sean was dressed in filmy black, which Nathaly declared was lovely, though Rosalee Atkins claimed anybody could see it was skimpy in the skirt.

The girls who could be gathered from the high school choir were present to sing a medley, and Mr. Cartwright, the only man there unless you counted Ullus Wingo, opened the program with an invocation to 'the Composer of the greatest music of all, the music of the spheres.'

Then Nathaly, in her lavender chiffon, introduced Mrs. Sean, 'who needs no introduction.'

Mrs. Sean walked to the front of the auditorium. The whispers mounted and stilled. She turned at the piano to face the group assembled.

'Miss Tatum tells me to speak a few words, but I am not fluent in that language, so I speak to you in one I know.'

They were amazed. They expected to hear an unknown tongue. But she turned, seated herself at the piano, adjusted the stool—a procedure that gained the rapt attention of the whole audience—and then began to play.

Ullus Wingo listened, and Dodo and the child, the preacher with a reverent expression, and Nathaly Tatum, wondering in dismay if she were hearing Bach, shocked at her lack of foresight in failing to insist on a printed program, realizing that she would not dare to thank Mrs. Sean for fear it was not he, and suffering throughout the performance the loss of such an opportunity. The others chose this time to discuss in whispers Mrs. Sean's halting words, all but the back rows, which were shocked to silence when Louella appeared at the church door, beneath the legend WELCOME ALL WHO ENTER HERE, and stood in the vestibule, listening.

When the concert was over, Nathaly hurried to the platform, clapping all the way down the aisle, and led

Mrs. Sean toward the church parlors for the reception that was to follow, expressing voluble appreciation 'on the part of each and every one present' for the delightful performance.

But the ladies were not at all satisfied with the evening. Katrine Sean did not talk about her daughter as any mother might be expected to talk, nor was she led to mention the dead husband, in whom they were particularly interested, having agreed that from the looks of the picture he must have been a good bit older than she. When Nathaly thought to ask her where on earth she'd learned to play like that, she did answer that she'd been her husband's pupil. At this the ladies exchanged glances, but, because they did not quite know what looks to wear, the glances were unsatisfying. And Dodo took them all away before the reception was good and started, took Mrs. Sean, the child, and Ullus Wingo. On the curb they were joined by Louella, who was wearing a white dress and shoes and a ribbon in her smoky hair. After that, Agnes Wingo, Ullus' mother, found herself the center of the group, a spot so unfamiliar to her that she bowed her gray head, clasped her chafed, pinpricked hands together, and said over and over again, 'I don't know what's come over my poor boy. I just don't know.'

Parky Osburn, from the bank, who'd had that day her first glimpse of the Seans, leaned against the wall, her ankles, in the girl-scout oxfords she always wore, crossed carelessly, and said in her booming voice,

'Well, for my money they're darn nice folks.' She faced them all, not challenging, with her punch glass gripped like a soft ball in her big red hand.

Nathaly would have been the first to say that she could never hate anyone. And this would have been an honest self-evaluation, for hate requires passion, and passion Nathaly had none. But she harbored a feeling of distinct distaste for Parky Osburn, for her cropped-off wind-blown hair, her bitten nails, her large knuckles. Nevertheless, it was from Parky Osburn that Nathaly's opinions came. Because Parky liked mountain vacations, Nathaly was of the opinion that mountains were not so relaxing as the shores of oceans; because Parky talked of sports—golf, tennis, hiking—Nathaly scorned physical prowess and could speak with such eloquence as breeding allows upon the satisfaction of hearths, 'good' books, Sunday afternoons upon her lavender chintz sofa. Because on their infrequent luncheon excursions together Parky unfailingly ordered French fries, steak, and fritters, Nathaly grew most fond of salads and abhorred fried foods categorically. Now that Parky had spoken, Nathaly knew at last her opinion of the Seans. She spoke, looking out the door through which the Seans had disappeared. 'It's been hard for me to identify the feeling I've had about them, but I believe—I do believe—it is *uneasiness*. Yes, it is a distinct feeling of uneasiness.'

And while she continued to muse, her eyes upon the door, she heard the word pass through the group like a little wind whispering through saplings. She had identified it for the whole assembly. They all avowed they'd felt it too.

Martin Lawrence, though he was seventeen years old and six feet tall, did not play on the basketball team. No appeals to his honor, his pride, his Chickasaw High spirit, could force him. And because his father was coach of a losing team, had himself once been a state champion, and should have been able to expect a son to follow suit, Martin was first a subject of puzzlement, then of scorn. He, too, listened to the music that afternoon, listened from under the wild clematis outside the church windows. Nobody knew he was there. Nobody ever knew where he was. When sometimes he was seen walking in alleys or across the fields, his wanderings were whispered about. But only he knew his quest; only he knew of the verses carried in a worn leather accounting book inside his shirt. The verses were about the people of the town. Had they known, they would have recognized as fear the disquieting bud in their breasts, not bloomed because seventeen-year-old boys do not yet deserve fear.

He knew the town as he had no right to know it. He did not know why he put his findings down in words. He never wondered. That night after the concert he presented himself at the open french doors of the Currer house. Dodo started. Mrs. Sean laid down her book. People thought him shy, but this night he spoke up readily enough.

'I never heard anything like that before,' he said. He

looked at Mrs. Sean, ignoring Ullus Wingo, Dodo, and the child. 'I'd like to hear some more.'

She studied him for a moment, smiled, and with a gesture invited him to come in.

The next day was the Fourth of July. There was a picnic in the park, a picnic with fireworks at dark. But it was not as ebullient as other picnics on Chickasaw Fourths had been. The Seans, Louella, Ullus Wingo, and Martin Lawrence had been seen early in the dawn packing the open car with lunches, thermos, bathing suits, and hats. They drove away toward the beach, leaving Chickasaw Cross to wonder. When the ladies discussed this turn of events at the picnic, Mate Atkins advised, 'If you all plan to catch that one, you'd best try shaking some salt on her tail.' And braying, he offered his services.

After that the Seans had no more callers. 'We'll just leave them to themselves,' the town said. But the town soon grew to feel that *it* was being excluded, though the piano played each day longer than the day before, Dodo went to market as she had before, and the child danced her laughing dance in the garden, watched over still by Ullus Wingo. They paid the town no mind but a smile and a nod. These the town found odious.

One mealtime when Martin Lawrence walked home from the Currer place, he met Jake McGowen on the sidewalk in front of Milton Pickett's drygoods store. Jake McGowan was Dade Lawrence's center, the tragic star of the losing team, and Dade had said on more than one occasion that Jake would be a son to make any father proud. Martin nodded and passed, but Jake stopped.

'See you found yourself a girl, Martin,' he said.

'What girl?'

'Why, the high yella. Ain't you the sly one.'

Martin Lawrence studied the rosy cheeks, the bristling haircut, the knowing smile, while Jake waited for the shrug he'd come to expect. Then a surprising thing happened: Martin began to laugh. Jake's smile dissolved. And while the laugh coughed in his chest, drew him like a cramp, Martin clapped a hand on Jake's shoulder. Jake knocked it off and crouched to fight.

'Oh, come on, Jake,' Martin said. 'I got no call to fight with you.'

At this, Jake swung. The blow struck Martin's rising arm. Then there was a fight that beat any the town had seen all year. Afterwards, to the surprise of every bystander, you couldn't really have said Jake took home any prize.

The night at supper Dade Lawrence smiled down upon his son, piled more meat on his plate. 'What'd I tell you, Mother? Chip off the old block. Boy didn't surprise me with the stuff he's made of. Yessir, can't keep a good man down. I knew it. I knew it all along. That's Dade Lawrence's boy, I tell you. And come next year he'll make All-State Forward or I'll throw in with you. Yessir. Old Jake and him tested each other out. What'd he say to you, boy, that got

131

you riled? Think you and him can hold the fort? Lord, there'll be no stopping the two of them. Lemme feel that muscle. Boy! We got our work cut out for us. What'd old Jake say to you, son, that made you fight? Oh well, I'll find out. I'll have to, for it's sure a charm.'

Martin ate his supper silently, allowed his arm to be bruised with probing fingers, spread a thin mask of a smile over his face. After dinner he kissed his mother at the kitchen door and went back to the Currer place.

Nathaly Tatum watched him pass her window. She rose to see him to the end of the block. Her book had dropped to her side; now she glanced down at it and let it fall. 'My, it's hot,' she said to the silent room. Outside, bumblebees tasted the larkspur. A big black fellow clung to a willow switch and cleaned himself. She knelt on the cushioned window seat and watched him put out his proboscis and scrape it with a feeler. Then he combed pollen from beneath his wings, one at a time, slowly, thoroughly, as he clung to the willow wand. 'I declare,' she said. 'Takes his time. Not like the hummingbirds, scared little things.'

'Hi there, Nat. What on earth you doing?' It was Parky Osburn.

'Oh, nothing much, I guess.'

'I'm going to the show. Want to come? It's Technicolor.'

'Oh—no, no thanks. I've a million things to do.'

'Well, so long then.' Parky waved.

Nathaly watched her whistle down the block, and her father's voice came back to her, 'whistling girls and crowing hens.' Nathaly wandered outside, ran her palm along the prickly hedge top. The mimosa had folded its leaves, though there was daylight yet. She'd heard that if you scrape a rib, the leaves will open again. She ran her fingernail along a rib and watched. The leaves still clung together. She turned to the willow, but the bee had gone. She hadn't realized that piano music had been playing, but now it stopped and she heard the cicadas in the silence. A bullfrog croaked from the creek bank across the road.

Nathaly passed through the gate and meandered down the walk. From the corner she could see the Currer place. There were people in the garden. It looked like a regular party. Then she saw that Parky Osburn had stopped at the fence, was leaning over it. Nathaly heard the laugh, the unrestrained, boisterous laugh. Hoyden, she thought. She'd torn off the mimosa frond and now her fingers, unknown to her, shredded it. Her pulse, her heart, the whole of her was beating. Her throat felt full and warm, as if she might be sick. Then Parky Osburn walked on toward the town. The forces in Nathaly relaxed. She could hear Parky whistling again. She turned back to her own house, went inside and to her bedroom.

The light was not on, but she could see herself, though not clearly, in the mirror. The shadowy self facing her was like a stranger, not like any mortal she had seen. She remembered standing before the same mirror as a child, frightening herself by moving close, closer, seeing the pupils of her own eyes pull closed like a draw-string purse. She'd thought first that the eyes held a strange being behind them, closed and hidden against herself. Then she saw her pupils as black holes into an empty darkness. 'When I die,' she thought—it was the first time the thought had framed itself in words. 'When I die they'll put a placard on the house and open it to garden tours.'

Her hand darted to flick on the lamp and, in passing, brushed the slender bottle of Opalescence to the floor. Her fingers did not proceed to the switch, and, standing, the shadow face still before her, she smelled the scent, too strong, too sweet, rise up from the broken bottle on the floor. Then Nathaly sat down at the window and cried, softly, as she couldn't remember crying even at her father's funeral. And she thought, How silly, to cry over a broken bottle.

After Martin left home that night, Dade Lawrence moseyed down to the drygoods store. For two purposes. He wanted to sit around drinking beer in the feed room with the men and brag about the fight, and he wanted to find out the charm—what it was Jake McGowan had said to Martin to make him fight.

And he did find out. He hadn't had a chance to finish his first beer before they told him.

'Jake was kidding him about the nigger gal,' Milt Pickett said. 'I don't know just how it come about, but Jake was teasing him about hanging around those new people at the Currer place—making out it was the nigger gal he was after.'

Dade tried to act himself, but by the time he finished the beer he'd broken into a sweat. On his way home he retched it all—beer and dinner—into the creek. At home, he went into the garage and took his whisky bottle down from the rafters. He sat in the driver's seat of his automobile and drank.

Very late, when Martin came home, Dade was waiting for him at the kitchen table. 'Where you been, son?'

'Out.' Martin shrugged.

'Don't give me none——' Dade started, then stopped, looking at the boy's face. 'Is it the gal, son? The colored gal?'

Martin plunged his hands into his pockets and turned away.

'You don't have to tell me how it is, son. Old Dade understands. Commere.' He motioned Martin to sit at the table. Reluctantly the boy dropped down. Dade put his arm about his son's shoulders. 'Look ahere, son, I know all about how it is. We got more in common than I ever thought.' He chuckled. Clumsily he patted Martin's arm. 'But not that one, son. Hear me? Not that particular one.'

Martin turned and looked at his father's eyes. But Dade looked away and fiddled with the salt cellar on the table. Then he forced himself to smile at the boy, a smile of shaky bravado.

'Hell, I don't give a hoot who you fool around with, you know that. Only—not the yella one. Now I don't want to hear any more about it, you understand?'

Martin sat looking at his father until Dade turned his face away. Then he got up. The chair fell over behind him and the noise exploded through the silent house, covering the sound of Martin's sob. 'I understand, *Father*.' The clumsy emphasis surprised and embarrassed him. He walked to the door and stood looking out the screen into the dark.

Dade let his forehead tip to rest on his fist upon the table. 'You'll play ball, won't you, son?'

Martin laughed.

'The team needs you, son. I need you. I need a winning squad this year. I don't know how much longer I can go on losing.'

Martin spread his fingers on the screen and shoved the door open. But he let it close again in front of him.

Nathaly remembered always the details of that August day. She remembered that in the morning she'd walked into Milton Pickett's just behind Louella, who grasped a shopping list in her hand. A woman at the notions counter dropped a card of pearl buttons, and Louella stopped, picked them up, smiled at the woman, and went on. Nathaly remembered that.

She remembered seeing Dodo in the afternoon walk along the creek bank calling the child. And just at dusk the boy, Martin Lawrence, passed through the alley as she emptied the garbage pail. He asked her if she'd seen the child. She had not.

It was daylight yet when Milton Pickett and Mate Atkins hustled up the block in front of her house. She was in the garden pruning hips from her roses so they might bloom again. And they told her that the child had disappeared, had not been seen since morning. And Milton Pickett added that Ullus Wingo was nowhere to be found. The men looked at each other, avoided looking at Nathaly. And as they walked away down the block, stopping at certain doors where they were joined by other men, Nathaly sat on the glider in her yard and had a hot flash.

The street was unnaturally quiet. The children who usually tumbled in the yards early on the summer nights or flew about the lawns chasing lightning bugs were nowhere to be seen. Women talked in low voices over fences, and Rosalee Atkins agreed with Mrs. Cartwright on the telephone that it was a judgment. Someone recalled a crime of passion in Rodgersville the summer before and it was recounted in brutal detail. They never found out who did it either. By nine o'clock a crowd had gathered in the Atkins yard.

Nathaly Tatum had watched for as long as she could from her own yard. Finally she walked down the street to stand on the fringe of the assembly. Mate Atkins was speaking from his top step. 'Let's do this up right, men, shipshape, hear me! Sheriff Pickett will take a group north through the pine woods toward Sommerset; Nate Hodges and Ben Lee Williams'll lead the Eagle Scouts through the marshes. I'll take those of you who're wearing gaiters into the swamp. Two pistol shots'll mean come in. Got that?'

Then out of the mob Agnes Wingo ran toward the Sean house crying out. Dodo appeared on the porch. 'Whatever he's done, it's your fault, do you hear me?'

Dodo looked at Agnes Wingo, at the people now overflowing the Atkins yard into the street. She said, 'If I could stop you, I would. But I cannot. So, I beg, do no violence. The child, we are not frightened for.'

The murmur of woman's outrage rose to a peak. Then the three groups separated, each to its captain, and Mate Atkins shouted, 'Heave to, you men, and remember, two shots brings you home.'

The women looked after the men departing. Children clung to their skirts, wide-eyed. Nathaly Tatum went to Agnes Wingo where she stood in the Sean yard and turned her away. She took her to the three-room clapboard house where she'd lived and sewed for the town for years. She did not speak, just sat with the old woman and listened to her mutter.

'I've done my best by him. The Lord gave me my cross and I bore it. Sometimes, when I look at him, I think it's a bad thing I dreamed. He looks like anybody else's boy when he's asleep. But I told myself, here is my sin to look at every day of my life. In my heart I hoped to bear it all—all of it. I thought the worst had happened and I'd done with it. But what's to happen now? What's to happen now?'

The night was long and, some maintain, unnaturally bright. Others said it was just that many were awake to see the moon run its course. It was not a full moon, but a new one with the old in its lap. And this was whispered to be an omen of evil. A ground fog crept from the swamp to invade the town, so that trees, houses, the forms of those who walked abroad seemed to float in members above the earth.

Some of the high-school girls stayed up all night down on the old courthouse square. Chickasaw Cross was once the county seat before the courthouse burned and was rebuilt over in Rodgersville. The old columns still stand, cracked and crumbling, in the square. The girls built a fire and kept coffee going all night for the men, should they return. You could see them from a distance, leaning against the old columns or huddled together, whispering. And once they forgot the terror of the occasion and broke into a campfire song. But someone soon put a stop to that. So they built up the fire and sat silent, looking into it. They, in fact, built the fire so high that Agnes Wingo, who could re-member the night the courthouse burned, looked out her window and fell to muttering, thinking she'd seen a revelation. For the fire licked against the columns just as it had that other night. And she re-called it was said the courthouse burned the night of the day an innocent man was hanged there in the square.

Nathaly held the old woman's quaking shoulders and tried to quiet her. But she rocked, muttering and moaning. Then she slept a little and woke screaming, 'They've hung him. See! The courthouse is on fire.'

Daylight was dawning when Mate Atkins led his weary searchers home. He stood in the street before the Sean house to fire the pistol shots. Some of the women had gone home. Those who'd stayed came out of the Atkins house, hurrying to see. Rosalee Atkins ran into the street, grabbed Mate's arm. He didn't look at her, just shook his head.

Nathaly Tatum ran all the way from the Wingo house across town, came in time to see the door of the Currer house open and Katrine Sean walk onto the porch. She stood while from the swamp the men straggled. They waited silently while from east and west the others came, Milt Pickett and Nate Hodges and Ben Lee Williams. One by one they walked to Mate Atkins there in the street where the first light of day, not strong enough yet to cast shadows, seemed to rise up from the dew-wet ground. They questioned each other, shook heads. When they'd all come, all accounted, they turned toward the woman on the porch. Dodo had come to stand beside her, with Louella in the dark of the doorway behind.

Mate Atkins raised his voice. 'You hear? We've searched the livelong night. They've not been found.'

Now from up and down the street the women were coming to crowd against the fence. Mate Atkins and Milton Pickett and Ben Lee Williams edged inside the gate. The crowd pressed closer. A section of the fence gave, sagging slowly, the wood cracking and splintering.

Katrine Sean spoke. 'You have done what you felt you must. Now, I plead, go home to your beds.'

One of the women cried out, 'It's unnatural. You, the child's mother! How can you stand there?'

Nathaly Tatum forced her way through the crowd. Her voice was shrill but she could not herself hear it, for her head was full of the voice of Agnes Wingo. 'I don't know what you've brought to this town,' she said. 'Whatever has happened,' and now she repeated the words that still rang in her head, 'it's your fault. It's you who will suffer—if you can suffer. And it's only just and right. He can't be held responsible.' She turned to the crowd of armed men and repeated, 'He can't be held responsible.'

The sun was rising now over the swamp, casting its yellow light over the marshes. Then, behind them, from the swamp, the crowd, then silent with a breath-sucked silence, heard the sound of music—piccolo, birdsong, they couldn't tell what. One by one they turned.

Across the creek, in the marshy field, they saw them walking, Ullus Wingo and the child, he with a reed flute, playing, the child sleepy, rubbing her eyes with her fist, skipping to keep up with his long stride. The people watched, the silence held, while they descended the slope, disappeared into the creek-bottom ravine, and then reappeared, heads first, as they mounted the near bank.

The crowd parted to let them through. Ullus Wingo hid the flute in the bib of his overalls and looked about him at the people as he walked. But the child went straight, not turning even her head, toward her mother there on the porch.

Then the two of them stood before her. The crowd was still. Katrine Sean stepped a step lower. Her hand hesitated just before touching the child, hovered above the child's head as she spoke. 'Where have you been?'

And the child said, for all in the dawn to hear, 'In the swamp the birds sing the livelong night. When you kick your feet in the water it lights like fire. There are trees with shapes like people and they moan when the wind blows. And he can make music, *Maman*, on a stick without a middle. And I believe it might be magic.'

For a moment that stretched out long, Katrine Sean looked down at the child's face. Then she raised her eyes and looked at the people.

Silently those nearest began to back away. A hand reached hurriedly and tried to right the broken fence. A voice said, 'Yes, but how do you know? You can't tell me——' But they backed away, watching, and one by one they turned and went in silence.

The sun was rising. Things heard in the dawn receded already, receded with the crowd to scatter into bits that lost themselves behind individual doors.

Nathaly Tatum was the last to go. She had collapsed against a fence post there near the walk. And there she leaned, her fist to her mouth, her eyes upon the spot where the child had stood. It was Parky Osburn, on her way to open the bank, who found her there. She had slept soundly all night long. She stopped on the walk, peered at Nathaly through her horn-rimmed spectacles, and said, 'Good gracious, Nat, you'll catch your death of cold.'

Not long after, they left—the three Seans and Louella. Ullus Wingo left too, for his mother finally agreed to have him put away to till the fields at the state home for the mentally retarded. The town insisted it was best, and they hid him away where they'd nevermore have to look at him. Then, early in the fall, Martin Lawrence went away too. Just went away. No one knew exactly when he left. They just realized one day that he was no longer there. Nathaly dropped membership in all the clubs of which she had been president and stayed home to tend her flowers. The chintzes faded in her house and she never replaced the bottle of Opalescence. She tended her roses and watched the hummingbirds that came in the warm evenings to the cluster of fading larkspur outside her bay windows. She sat for the hours of twilight, watching the hummingbirds hover, hesitate, and dart nervously to taste the sweet, still mystery of the flower, then spurt backwards, fearful, hovering on frantic wings, and then sneak a taste again, in the twilight.

And soon the Seans became a legend—like the story of the Pied Piper—told on dusk-dark verandahs amid pipe smoke and the click of needles. Everyone knew the tale by heart and told it. They told it over and over, to themselves only, never to strangers, for it was private and of the town. As if it contained a riddle to be solved, they waited each time it ended to hear if someone might speak up. And many a child went to sleep in the dark and the silence, waiting.

BENNY RICCO'S SEARCH FOR TRUTH

B ENNY RICCO, a good Catholic all his life, found it increasingly difficult, once his saintly mother died and left him on his own, to drag himself out of bed for early Mass. St. Paul's, in close proximity, woke him with its bells, and opening his eyes he could see its spires through the window. But he found that by closing the window he spared himself the alarum of the bells, and by pulling his yellow shade he could shut out the sense of it altogether.

She had not been one month in her grave before he began to reflect upon the reason for the slight attendance on weekday mornings: Mass is, after all, required only on Sundays. Though his conscience, his most energetic part, put in objections, he gave up going at all on the other six days of the week. He reasoned that, as he was a working man and never left the hotel until almost midnight, he needed his sleep. For a time his old mother railed at him, but it was agreeable to find himself out of her reach. And she soon shut up.

He imagined that, taken up with the joys of Heaven, she had forgotten him, her son. His feeling of neglect soon turned to a feeling of relief not unfamiliar to him. Once, while in high school, he had hawked popcorn at the municipal auditorium when the feature attraction was a Scots band in kilts, playing bagpipes. The noise, the raillery of the pipes, had led him to abandon the wire tray three quarters filled with unsold wares, and, arms over ears, seek refuge from the awful sound in the catacombs beneath the bleachers. The relief he had felt to be out of their reach was not unlike this relief he now felt at finding himself beyond reach of the old woman's voice. Now he could do as he liked. He could, if he wanted to, drink a can of beer with his midnight supper. And spared the rigors of the daily communicant, he could eat what he liked and when he liked. He grew forgetful and, eating out as he did, one thing led to another until often he had hamburgers, his favorite meal, even on Friday. Nothing struck him down for it, and he grew a bit cavalier in his attitudes, being jerked up only once a month now when he betook himself, full of guilt, to confession.

Usually he was the first in line, the first to have it over. He'd say his penance at the rail and be out before the line was long in front of the yellow oak box. But one Saturday he was late, having sat twice through a horror movie. The priest, Father Verciglio, had been hearing for two hours and was waiting for his relief, young Father Donadio, to come along so he could go and eat his supper. When Benny Ricco, heavy with

146

shame, sidled in and knelt, blessed himself, began, the exhausted priest covered his lips and yawned.

That experience gave more relief to Benny Ricco than a hundred penances set end to end. He saw that Father Verciglio was, after all, just a tired man who listened to catalogues of sin as no more than his job, and that he, Benny Ricco, was of no great importance to him. After that he grew slovenly in his confessions, learning the art of phraseology. 'Father, I ate meat on Friday.' That was enough. What did it matter, a bite or a pound, one Friday or four in a row? He got the same penance, five Our Fathers and five Hail Marys, and the same absolution. And he told himself that his sins were likely nothing, practically virtues in comparison with the horrors, outrages, the priests must hear in the dark of their Saturday afternoons.

Once young Father Donadio, not long in the parish, came to a luncheon at the hotel. Seeing him cross the lobby, Benny stepped forward to speak. But the priest's eyes showed no recognition. At first Benny thought the priest had snubbed him for his laxity, and he knew the luxury of righteous indignation. But then he realized that the new assistant had forgotten his face, had honestly failed to recognize him. This was worse. It filled him with fear and loneliness. He took his dinner hour early, went to the deserted church, and made the stations of the cross alone. Afterwards he felt better and sitting in a front pew, he made some promises.

But the knowledge of the priest's empty gaze upon him, as though he'd been just another Protestant, soon took on new significance. As he'd first been grieved at the neglect of his sainted mother, the grief soon turning to relief, now the neglect of Father Donadio also occasioned relief. He broke the promises he had made and nothing struck him down. He began to feel like a free agent. He pondered the meaning of free will and came to his own conclusions.

A solitary young man, Benny Ricco lived alone now in the rooms above the antique dealer's shop. He rose at noon, ate his breakfast, and dressed in his uniform for work. He liked uniforms, in fact wore this one off duty as well as on, and for that reason he'd been disappointed when the army turned him down as unfit because of his weak eyes. He'd decided later that it was just as well, for the army sent you to far places and made you stand in the sun or peel potatoes. His hotel uniform was blue, a more becoming color to him anyway, and as fancy as an officer's. And it served as well as any to signify that he belonged to something.

As he was a vain young man, he spent a good deal of time each day before the mirror, combing his hair and patting it with a perfumed dressing. He knew he had good looks—black curly hair falling over a slanting forehead, olive complexion, regular features, and dark eyes that, if they looked weak, also looked large and round and appealingly innocent, like the eyes of a child. Moreover, though not so tall as he would like to be, he was well-built, as the short-jacketed uniform disclosed. But he knew also that such good looks are

common among Italian youths. He would have been
a rarer bird if his name were Smith. He'd made up
his mind that if he ever moved from this neighborhood
and changed jobs to another hotel, he would call himself by another name. He'd discarded Mark, David,
Morris, all of which appealed, for fear he'd be taken
for a Jew. Finally, he'd decided on Robert. He liked
the sound so much that he compounded it to Robert
Robertson. No dago, no wop, had ever been called
from the cradle Robert Robertson. As Robert Robertson, he felt he might go far. Once, for a time, he had
imagined himself being discovered by a talent scout
and carried off to Hollywood. These imaginings lasted
only a short while, but long enough for the purchase
of a guitar. He had a good voice and had once, while
still a soprano, sung a solo in the boys' choir, looking
cherubic in black cassock and white surplice. This
vision of himself had led him, for a time, to contem-
plate the priesthood as a living. But the blue uniform
of the bellhop had brass buttons.

The fourth floor of the hotel was given over to residents—those people, occuring singly, who paid rent
by the month and lived in rooms jam-packed with
personal belongings, here a phonograph, there a
chiffonier. Mrs. Anderson kept a parakeet, and Miss
Frazer a Siamese cat. The natural animosity of these
pets occasioned constant ill-will between the ladies.
Mr. Singleton had a little dog that he walked three
times a day on a leash to the city park and back. There

was also Mr. Buzz Eckert, the insurance salesman who was separated from his wife; and Mr. Miles Baumgartner, the bachelor drug salesman, who made this his headquarters though his territory carried him over the north central part of the state. For the most part the residents were elderly retired people who lived there maybe a few months, then went to relatives, county homes, hospitals, or government housing as their income ran out. These five stayed.

Benny Ricco had little to do with them. Once daily he removed Miss Frazer's box of kitty litter and emptied it in the alley, for she was a good tipper and made it worth his while. He came in contact with them more often on the rare occasions when he had to tend the elevator if one of the regular boys got sick. Elevator duty, he resented. He'd begun as an elevator boy working after school, but he'd moved up to the permanent position, better paid and with the added attraction of tips, when he graduated. He did not doubt that some day he would be bell captain. And from there he intended to go higher, moving to a chain hotel where ultimately he might hope to become room clerk, learn the business, go to night school, and one day be a manager. Part of him knew this ambition to be made of the stuff of dreams, the other part clung to it as certain reality.

Soon after the memorable days of Father Verciglio's yawn and Father Donadio's neglect, Benny Ricco carried into the elevator two good leather suitcases, preceded by the gentleman to whom they belonged, a man tall, cadaverous, hollow-eyed and hollow-cheeked, wearing a raincoat over his shoulders like a cape and a brown hat with its wide brim turned down, meeting his turned-up collar behind, shading his eyes in front.

Benny led him to 403, recently vacated by the death, in hospital, of a former resident, a Mrs. Jenkins. The room had been vacant for over a week. Mr. Thomas, Benny surmised, would not be permanent, for he'd brought along too little, not even his own bedside radio. Most of the other residents kept radios going all day long and were especially interested in the weather. They also, particularly the ladies, had a tendency to leave the doors to their rooms open and call back and forth to each other. As Benny led Mr. Thomas down the hall, the ladies, he knew, were watching. Miss Frazer came to her door wearing her eggshell silk lounging pajamas and took this opportunity to call 'Kitty-kitty-here-kitty-kitty' to the Siamese cat, who had draped itself over the boxed exit light to the fire escape, a position that afforded both warmth and height of vantage. The cat looked down at Benny and the newcomer with malice in its strange pink eyes.

He unlocked the door, turned on the overhead light, and stood aside to let in the guest, who stalked past him, stood in the center of the room, and looked around. Benny set up the luggage racks and laid the bags upon them. He opened the window, turned on the bathroom light, and asked, 'Will that be all, sir?'

Mr. Thomas had moved up beside the bed and was

bending over the night table. Benny thought he might be looking up a number to telephone. But when the guest straightened and turned, Benny saw in his hand the red-backed Gideon Bible he'd removed from the drawer.

'Take this out of here,' Mr. Thomas said. For the first time Benny got a good look at him. The guest had the appearance of an ancient cadaver preserved by some secret drying process. Benny did not try to guess his age. The conclusion might have been preposterous.

He took the Bible and stood waiting for his tip. Mr. Thomas shrugged out of his trench coat, threw it on the chair, turned, 'Well?'

'Will that be all, sir?' Benny smiled expectantly.

'I am not in the habit of tipping,' Mr. Thomas said, his parchment lips seeming to take some pleasure in the words.

Benny Ricco bowed slightly from the waist, turned on his heel, and closed the door behind him. As he walked down the hall, Mrs. Anderson was standing in her door, the parakeet perched on her shoulder. She raised her eyebrows and nodded significantly as she espied the Bible under his arm.

'I'll take that,' she said. 'Mine disappeared and the management has failed to replace it. The service here is not what it used to be.'

Benny handed over the Bible and proceeded to the elevator.

'I do not think,' she called after him, loud enough for Miss Frazer to hear, 'that pets should be allowed the freedom of the corridors. I keep my Pepe in the room and others should do likewise in the interest of co-operation.'

When the elevator arrived and opened its doors, Benny stepped in, turned, and smiled at the lady. The cat, still draped over the exit light at the other end of the short hall, let its eyelids drop like veils as the elevator, behind the grillwork doors, descended.

As the newcomer was not a tipper, Benny lost interest in him. When he went for the kitty litter in the mornings, the door to his room was always closed. Miss Frazer once leaned and whispered explosively in Benny's ear as she pointed to the door, 'Something of a hermit. *I'd* say. You never see him in the dining room. *I* don't know how he keeps his strength up. Old Singleton says he looks like a man with a bad liver. Ought to take liver pills.' She snorted. 'I knew an old lady once took liver pills all her life.' She snorted again, poking two long stiff fingers into Benny's ribs. 'When she died they had to beat her liver to death.'

As he waited for the elevator, Mr. Singleton joined him with his dog, who sniffed at the box of kitty litter. It was a small pink-skinned pug-nosed bow-legged thing with a corkscrew tail like a pig's. 'Here, Max, stop that!' Mr. Singleton said in his small, waspish voice. The elevator came and they got in and whirred down to the lobby, where the dog's toenails clicked on the parquet floor. 'The new guest,' Mr. Singleton said, 'will he be long with us?'

Benny said he didn't know.

'He is a troubled man,' Mr. Singleton said. 'Up all hours of the night, pacing the floor *back* and forth, *back* and forth. Sometimes I have to rap on the wall or lose my sanity. It doesn't do any good though. Max hears him and whines. Between Thomas on the one side and Mr. Eckert's nightly domino game on the other, I hardly get any sleep any more.' And he passed out through the revolving door, the little dog scudding along beside him, while Benny disposed of the kitty litter and took up his stand against a pink marble column in the lobby, removing from inside his jacket the newspaper he pilfered daily from the self-service stand beside the cigar counter. He was selective in what he read, limiting his attention to stories of murder, suicide, kidnaping, robbery, and rape, following a crime from its appearance in front-page headlines until finally it occasioned an editorial calling for more rigorous law enforcement, indicating to Benny that the plot had reached its conclusion.

Coming out of the church after Mass on a Sunday morning, Benny saw the newcomer sitting on a bench in the park across the way. He sat as still as any of the park's statues, his brown hat pulled down, the raincoat draped over his shoulders though the early spring day was warm and sunny. He sat so still that the squirrels skittered back and forth in front of him and the pigeons waddled about his feet, unafraid.

While the homeward-bound congregation surged around him, Benny stood on the high top step and watched him there. He could only see the man's chin, and yet he had the feeling that Thomas was not looking at the ground as he seemed to be, but at the church. Benny had to pass the bench on his way to the hotel, which fronted on the opposite side of the park. But Thomas didn't look up even though a small boy sidled near and tried to peer into his face.

Then for another week Benny didn't set eyes on him. When he went into the church the next Sunday morning, the park bench was empty, but when he came out again, there was Thomas—same hat, cape, statuesque stillness, perhaps even the same squirrels and pigeons. And so it went, week after week, until one Sunday Benny remained standing on the top step while the congregation melted away and left him alone, confronting Thomas across the street. Then he walked down, crossed, and slowed as he approached the bench. The squirrels fled.

'Good morning, sir,' he said.

But Thomas did not answer, did not even look up.

In his agitation, with still an hour to kill before going on duty at noon, Benny hurried down the sidewalk that carried him to the center of town, called Five Points because five avenues converged there into a chaos of traffic that crept in a circle around a large fountain. He took up a stand under the great clock in the wedge-shaped corner of the city's largest department store. It was a favorite meeting place, where young men picked up mothers-in-law after church to take them home to Sunday dinner and sleepy parents swerved to the curb to pick up children after Sunday school. Benny stood, hands behind his back, and watched the slow cars dip to the curb, rear doors opening to scoop up the figures that scurried into them, barely safe before the motors roared them away. And he watched the faces of the strollers. He often stood and watched the faces going by. He had haunted the Five Points corner from the days of his childhood, when his presence there still had an urgency, long since lost. Though Antonio Ricco walked out of the rooms above the antique dealer's shop before Benny, his son, was born, Benny had been certain, as a child, that the face of this stranger, his father, was among those he passed in the street each day. He had felt that if he stood there long enough, on the Five Points corner, he would one day see him go by, and that when he did he would know him. And once he did see a face. His heart had leaped against the bars of its small prison, and he'd hurried after the retreating figure, gaining to try to glimpse the face, then falling back, afraid. The man at length ducked into an alleyway in the warehouse district. Benny almost ran to keep from losing him. When he rounded the corner, he bumped into the man waiting there, a scowl darkening the face, now strange and not at all the face Benny'd had in mind. He felt his mouth stretch into an anxious smile. Then his breath rushed out of him, his head snapped downward, and he was surprised to glimpse the wrist that had plunged a fist and buried it in his stomach. The face faded and there was only the hairy fist withdrawing, and Benny felt that it gripped his insides and tore them away. Then he saw the knee crook, jab, and fist, face, knee dissolved, the narrow canyon, the cobbled, stained, and rutted alley blotted out. Finally he awoke, his cheek pressing grit through a blob of spittle, his new uniform oil-marked and his body throbbing in waves of pain. Afterwards he no longer looked for any face. The experience was one he did not think about. Whenever the bare suggestion of the memory of it cast a shadow at the edge of the lighted part of his consciousness, he was likely to writhe as if he felt a sudden spasm, an itch, a pain. And the quick writhing was usually enough to rid him of the shadow.

He no longer looked for any face, but the habit of the corner was ingrained. And he often killed time there, waiting for whatever he had to wait for.

Immediately upon his return to the hotel, the switchboard girl beckoned to Benny and said that 403 was calling for him.

'For me in particular?' he asked, and added, 'Because if not, I've an errand and you can send somebody else.' It wasn't true. He merely wanted to know if Thomas had singled him out.

'He asked for you,' the girl said.

'I didn't think he knew my name,' Benny said, but this didn't rouse comment because the light on the board was flashing. He wondered if Mr. Thomas had asked for 'the Italian,' and concluded that he had. So he was filled with resentment by the time he confronted the door marked 403.

He knocked. Miss Frazer had come into the hall to watch.

'Come in,' Thomas barked from inside. And Miss Frazer drew down the corners of her lips and nodded as if this were precisely and significantly what she had expected.

Benny tried the door, found it unlocked. He opened it, went in, and stood just where the little corridor made by closet and bath gave upon the room itself.

Thomas was sitting with a leg crossed over his knee, looking sideways down from his window. The room was on the front of the hotel, and the view below was of the park. Across the intervening block, the spires of St. Paul's rose above the trees. Benny saw that the front doors were barely visible where the trees divided around a walk. Could Thomas see him enter there on Sunday mornings? Could he pick him out in his blue uniform, its brass buttons catching the sun? Unlikely. Still . . .

'You rang, sir?' he said.

Thomas turned his head, glanced at him, looked back out the window. Uncovered, his head proved to be topped by a coarse shock of black hair. Above his aged face, the hair looked like the hair on a corpse that persists in growing. Benny wondered if it were dyed. Thomas wore his sideburns long and curving. There were webs of wrinkles around his eyes, as if he'd spent a lot of time squinting at the sun. His lower face was brown as leather, but his high forehead was white and fragile above an indentation left by the wide-brimmed hat.

'I see you are a believer in the true religion,' Thomas said finally, his voice weighted with mockery. It was a low, hoarse voice like a whisper.

'I am, sir,' Benny said, his hands clasped behind him, waiting.

Thomas turned and studied him, his face expressionless. Then he said, 'I am curious about this particular manifestation of man's inordinate proclivity for self-deception.'

Benny, standing at parade rest, shifted his weight uneasily. Thomas' remark left him in the dark, a state he found distasteful. Moreover, though the meaning of the words was not clear, the tone was. He decided to make no comment.

Thomas nodded as though he approved Benny's silence. 'I am an archeologist,' he said, and Benny thought he had proclaimed himself a fortuneteller. 'I have delved into the history of *homo sapiens* as far as any man who ever lived, and I can assure you that he evolved from the ape and not from Adam, that a freak of nature, a fortunate mutation, left him equipped with an apposite thumb that gave him enormous advantage over his brothers in that it enabled him to wield a club, and from this ability evolved all the notions of man's superiority to beasts. So. How does it feel, Mr. Ricco, to know that the vulgar edifice confronting us there—' he glanced toward the church

159

spires—'based on assumptions of the divine essence, got its rise, as did all of civilization, from a genetic event no different in kind from that which produces two-headed calves?'

Benny did not answer, as he did not know what he'd been asked. But when Mr. Thomas waited, watching his face, Benny made himself say, 'I'm not sure I understand your question, sir.'

'Perfect! You don't understand a simple question, and yet you protest an understanding of the marvelous system upon which that architectural outrage is based. Amazing. Please explain.'

'Explain—sir?'

'Come. Draw up a chair. We'll not stand on formality. It can't be done in a minute.' He gestured toward St. Paul's. 'Rome wasn't built in a day, ha ha.'

But Benny said, 'I'm all right on my feet, sir.' He wanted very much to escape.

'And where will you begin?' Thomas asked, striking a match on the window screen and holding it to his cigar. The breeze took the white puff of smoke out the window where it disappeared.

'Begin, sir?' Benny asked. 'I'm not just positive I get the gist——'

But Thomas interrupted. 'I want you to explain to me why, on Sunday mornings, you betake yourself to that mock-Gothic pile of rock, dabble your fingers in contaminated water, listen to mumblings in a language you do not understand, make mysterious signs on your breast, bob, duck, and carry on in a manner becoming to the mentally deranged.'

Now Benny found himself, was able to rock a little on the balls of his feet, expand his chest, and smile assuredly. Now that he understood the question, he felt on solid ground. For all his unintelligibility, Thomas was likely just another Baptist trying to trick him. In the certainty of his position—a member born, chosen, baptized in the Mother Church—he felt suddenly quite erudite. He knew the catechism by heart, but more than that, he knew he was smiled upon, favored by the Most High over this infidel.

'I go to church on Sunday because it is a mortal sin if I do not,' he said, omitting the 'sir' because now he perceived that the interview had little to do with his position at the hotel.

'Oh? And what is mortal sin?' Thomas asked, spewing forth smoke into the close air of the room.

'If I died in a state of mortal sin, my soul would go to Hell,' Benny said.

'Soul? What is your soul? Have you ever seen it? Do you feel it palpitate? I have examined every organ, muscle, bone, every ounce of flesh, every tissue of the human body, and I have found no soul.'

Benny had to hold himself to keep from squirming. It was a question that had bothered him. He saw his soul like a clean oval bar of soap floating somewhere in his rib cage, but he knew that this was not an approved image. He reverted to his catechism. 'Naturally, sir,' he said. 'The soul is a spirit and immortal.'

161

'And if you commit sin, then die, you have condemned this—immortal soul, that God wants for himself in Heaven, to everlasting damnation in a place called Hell? Do I understand you?'

'That's about it, sir.' And Benny rocked on his toes, pleased with the clarity of his dialectic.

'Ah, Mr. Ricco, I find myself drawn to this religion of yours. Think what it makes of man. Your mere mortal self has dominion over the immortal, can thwart the will of God. Not even your whole self— just, let us say, your mouth which sends meat to your stomach on the fifth day of the week. This poor vulnerable soft muscle, the mouth, can condemn your immortal soul to Hell. This mere mortal self can thwart the will of the Almighty, can pluck the soul from His grasp and send it winging its way to Hell.' He chuckled, tapping ash from his cigar with his little finger.

Benny stopped rocking. 'Well, I wouldn't exactly say—I'd never thought of it in just that light, sir.' The idea was enormous. He could not immediately encircle it.

Mr. Thomas smiled at the cigar between his fingers. 'The magnitude of your intellect has tired me, Mr. Ricco. We'll continue our discussion some other time. You may go now.'

But Benny, far from breathing his sigh of relief, turned hesitantly, even paused a moment at the door before going out. 'Good day, sir,' he said, as he'd been taught to say by the manager. But Mr. Thomas, lost again in contemplation of St. Paul's steeple, did not answer.

Benny felt that he'd been made to appear foolish, a sensation he found particularly repugnant. His first thought was to confront the priest with the disturbing idea that had been lodged in his head, as much to have an answer for Thomas as to regain his own peace of mind. But again he saw Father Verciglio's yawn and Father Donadio's empty gaze.

So, instead, he took himself up the street to the public library. But once in the presence of so many books, he found himself at a loss. The librarian crept up to him in the reading room and announced her presence with a sibilant, odorous whisper. Starting, Benny turned. She stood a head taller than he, her pale hair done in small, tight springs that bounced with her every movement. The afternoon sun reflected off her rimless spectacles, so that in the place of eyes her head was equipped with dual rays surrounded by coils that gave the summit, the apex of her, an electrifying effect.

'Can I be of chervish?' she asked.

Benny started to speak but caught himself before he had disturbed the funereal silence.

'Could I chuggest a book?'

He nodded, reduced by her proprietary air.

She looked at the bookshelves in front of them. 'A novel?' She ran her long spatulate finger across the spines of a row of books until it slowed and stopped with all the inevitability of the needle on a gambling wheel. 'Thish, I highly recommend,' she exclaimed.

'What's it about?' Benny asked.

'Itch about a Russian family that runs a boarding house in China,' she said in her broadcast whisper. 'Shall I check it out?'

Despairing, Benny nodded. He left the library with the novel tucked under his arm. On his way back through the park, he came upon the cloaked statue sitting on a bench by the fountain. He tried to hurry past, but Mr. Thomas hailed him.

'Well, Ricco. I see you are literate. What's that you've got?'

Without speaking, Benny passed the book over to him.

Thomas read the title. 'Well-well,' he said. 'I suppose the Roman Index narrows the possibilities considerably.'

'I read what I like,' Benny said. 'It's a free country.'

'Oh ho! A budding humanist!' Thomas laughed.

The next day Benny went back to the library at his dinner hour. Looking about, he found his librarian nowhere in sight. With relief, he dropped the book in the chute and turned again to the shelves in the reading room.

Out of nowhere she materialized. 'My, aren't we a shpeedy reader,' she said, not without blame.

'Well, it wasn't *quite*, it wasn't *exactly* what I had in mind. What I'm looking for is actually a book—well —on the Index.'

'Indecsh?'

'Yes, you know—*forbidden*.'

164

'Oh-o-oh,' her voice rose and fell conspiratorially on the note. '*Verboten*. A philosophical treatish?'

'That's it,' he said.

'Um. Let me chee now. I can give you Kant, Shpinosa—no, he won't do. Nietzsche, Hegel, no Heidegger. Oh, take Chartre? Jean-Paul Chartre. Chartre and Kierkegaard!'

She paused triumphantly, and he nodded, caught up by her enthusiasm, thrilling suddenly with civic pride that his quest could be so efficiently served.

She went to the catalogue files, wet her thumb at her lip, flipped through the cards with gay abandon. Then she wrote swiftly, ripped the leaf with finality, handed it to a young girl in saddle shoes, and smiled up at him in the pride of accomplishment.

Soon he had two slim yellow volumes in his perspiring hand. Eager to escape, he was held by the woman with, 'I believe you are a deep and profound cheeker after truth.'

'It's just—I was wondering—' he began, a little frightened now, hoping to insist that he was not habitually given to heresy. But a bright, expectant smile awoke on her face and she put a hand to her hair.

Muttering a frantic farewell, he turned and hurried out, clutching the books in his hand.

Mr. Thomas was buying cigars when Benny entered the lobby. He touched the books under Benny's arm. 'What is it this time?' he asked.

'Chart!' Benny said with conviction.

Mr. Thomas laid back his head, laughed with more

vigor than he'd displayed heretofore, and betook his brittle bones to the elevator.

That night Benny unearthed his glasses and, at the kitchen table, under the glare of the naked overhead bulb, opened one of his books. Almost at once he found what he was looking for, what purported in the first sentence to answer the question of the soul. Eagerly he read, 'Man is spirit. But what is spirit? Spirit is the self. But what is the self? The self is a relation which relates itself to its own self, or it is that in the relation (which accounts for it) that the relation relates itself to its own self; the self is not the relation but (consists in the fact) that the relation relates itself to its own self.' Having gone thus far, Benny turned back and began again. But going backwards or forwards, he came upon more of the same.

First baffled, then enraged, he slammed the book closed and took up his newspaper. But he found himself too angered by the book to read anything. He would have returned it at once to the library, but he could not think with equanimity of meeting his librarian again just yet. So he left the books to lie there, offensive to his sight, on his kitchen table beside the abandoned guitar. They were still there the following Sunday morning when again he encountered Mr. Thomas in the park, this time before instead of after Mass.

The guest spoke genially enough and moved over to make room for him on the bench. Benny hesitated. Across the street the last of the congregation scurried through the portals. The unreadable books had suggested to Benny that there was more in Heaven and earth than his philosophy took into account, so, setting his jaw with the air of one braving the unknown, Benny Ricco sat down.

Mr. Thomas did not speak again until after the tolling of the last bell. Then he exhaled sadly, took out a cigar but left it unlighted, and sighed again. 'You are a great disappointment to me, Mr. Ricco,' he said.

But the words did not register with Benny. Surprised at his nerve, a little afraid, he watched the usher come and close the church doors, shutting him out.

Looking sadly at St. Paul's façade, Mr. Thomas said, 'In my youth I set out in search of Truth. Thinking perhaps I might find it buried in the past, I prepared myself by going seven years to a university in the East. And, still young, I found myself at last in the Valley of the Kings where I worked as a laborer for the British to uncover an Egyptian tomb. After twelve months, we succeeded and stood aside to witness the unwrapping of the inmost mystery.'

Benny caught his breath and turned from the church to his companion. 'What was it?'

'Death,' Thomas said. 'The sepulcher was empty. It was Death itself they had preserved. Death still stinking after more than three thousand years. There he was, the first true believer, the first who taught there was one God, the one who, some believe, was the teacher of Moses.'

The speaker grew silent, contemplating the toes of

his high-topped shoes. 'Later I worked on a tomb supposedly guarded by a curse. I hoped to die of it, but I did not.'

'Hoped to die!' Benny breathed.

'A curse would have been something. There was nothing. Another corpse.'

Benny's answer was silence.

Thomas said, 'In Germany, a young schoolmaster, on a bet, once set out to decipher cuneiform hieroglyphics which had been declared insoluble. He labored several years. I can imagine that, before he finished, he was convinced he was turning the key in the final door. Do you know what the tablets said? "Who with malice prepense destroys, effaces, or moves from its place this my signed attestation, may he be denounced by Ninmah before Bel, Sarrateia, his name, his seed in the land, may it be destroyed." ' Thomas laughed, quiet eruptions that shook his frame like sobs. ' "Look on my works ye mighty and bow down." Oh the pride, the folly of the human race.'

Then he stood up, bent his knees straight with his hands, grunted at the exertion, and began to walk away.

'Wait!' Benny called, rising after him, afraid suddenly to find himself alone.

Thomas did not turn or seem to hear. Benny watched him diminish down the walk. Then, as he faced the steeple, the enormity of his sin came upon him. He waited for the sky to cloud, the thunder to peal, the lightning to strike out. The sky remained bland and blue, the sun smiled upon him. It was as if God, like Father Verciglio, had yawned.

Forgotten of God, Benny Ricco wandered for a time, forlorn. But gradually he grew in pride to accept his freedom. Now he left his window up, his shade unpulled, and every morning he was rewarded by a moment of truth.

His only regret was that Thomas no longer took any notice of him whatsoever. Once when Benny tried to force his attention, Thomas looked up from his seat in the lobby, his face like leather sagging on its frame, and said, 'Go away, young man. I am old, can't you see? I have many things to think about before I die.'

'I'd like to hear some more about the—about Egypt,' Benny persisted. 'I plan to do some traveling myself one day.'

Thomas said, 'I was born in this town and I will die in it. Travel is no great matter.'

'I want to see for myself,' Benny said.

'No man does that any more, boy.'

'I once went with the nuns to the state capital,' Benny said. 'We saw the house of Jefferson Davis. But he was not there. He was dead.'

'Did you travel a hundred miles to discover that? Leave me alone, young man, or I'll complain to the management. Good Lord! And I said to myself, "Out of the mouths of babes"— You are as empty as my tombs.'

Angered and dismayed, Benny turned away.

The following morning the room clerk met him coming in. 'Go see if the maids are finished in four-oh-three,' he said. 'I have a new resident waiting.'

'But,' Benny said, a cold fist clutching his vitals, 'Four-oh-three is occupied.'

'He's gone. He won't be back.'

'Where did he go?'

'To St. Vincent's in the night.'

'Sick! He's sick?'

'He's sick all right. He went in the ambulance.'

Benny Ricco rushed into the street. There was no taxi at the stand, so he began to run in the direction of the hospital. It stood on a rise outside of town, a mile away.

He arrived, winded, and stood panting furiously in the face of the nursing nun on duty. They confronted each other for minutes before he could choke out the name. Her eagle bonnet flounced as she scanned her book. 'Second floor, west,' she said.

He turned and ran.

She looked up. 'Wait, young man!'

But Benny, ignoring the elevator, was on the stairs. Outside the room he paused, straightened his tie, put his hand through his hair. He pushed in the door.

The room was empty, the bed stiffly made, the covers tucked and straining on the narrow mattress. The sun fell on the single window, blinding him.

In the afternoon paper he found the obituary. Vergil Thomas, aged 70, born, lived, died in this city, for forty years a postal clerk, upon retirement joined his daughter in St. Louis, recently returned to make his home at the San Sebastian Hotel.

'Hah!' he said, but he felt no real elation. He felt, instead, he was on an elevator whose mechanism had gone wild, first lifting him up, up, until any moment the walls might drop away and himself in the fragile cage shoot skyward, all life revealed, spread out beneath him, patterned, orderly. But before that august moment it shuddered to a halt, hung tenuous upon its cables, then plummeted. The floor fell away and left him falling free inside the cage, his stomach and lungs crushed in deceleration by the weight of his falling bones and flesh.

As summer deepened toward its still, dead center, Benny Ricco found himself in the grip of a strange phenomenon. He could not read the newspaper; but neither could he escape from it. From the stand on the corner it screamed at him. Murder! Robbery! Rape! And he wanted to hide himself in the telephone booth with the door almost, but not quite, closed, so that the light would not come on. Yet he found he could not escape so easily, for the sight of the telephone itself awoke in him strange yearnings. He was afraid he might place a call to the police and confess to everything. Murder. Robbery. Rape. It was he. The guilty.

He no longer returned to his lonely room but walked the empty streets at night where candy wrappers scuttled down alleyways before the wind.

Small in the canyon he walked, a furtive figure, after the neon signs had bubbled out, when street lights paled to merge into the dawn. Or for hours he stood, watched only by the street light's pale moon, under the silent, moving clock on the Five Points empty corner, hearing only the splash of the dark fountain. Then again he walked. And beside him, behind him, before him walked a figure he could not see, whose footsteps hid themselves in the echo of his own, a ghost bent on revenge, a restless soul without its peace, by turns accusing him and begging his forgiveness.

Each morning he found himself beached by the wind before a square red brick building with a single globe of light like the center globe of a pawnbroker's sign suspended over the door. And finally he went in, causing a mild sensation.

He stood at the base of a dais occupied by a blue-jowled, white-haired arbiter and found himself a bone contended by two plain-clothes champions of the law, standing one on either side of him. Their voices were close, but when he looked at the speakers their figures blurred at the distant end of his tunnel of vision.

'Listen,' said the one who seemed to be his prosecutor. 'How come you don't confess to one still on the books? I got that one solved. Listen, I had enough trouble. The guilty man's in jail, waiting on his trial.'

'Crice!' said the other, who regarded Benny with a proprietary air, 'You don't have nothing. What you got? Circumstantial evidence.'

'My man's a confirmed criminal,' said the first, with

pride. 'This guy's a crackpot. I can spot them a mile off. What're you after, anyway, my job?'

'I'm after the truth,' said Benny's champion. 'What I'm after is the truth, the whole truth, and nothing but the truth.'

'Well, get the machine then. If it's truth you're after, bring in the machine!'

Then the voices seemed to Benny to recede and echo from a point as distant as the figures themselves. The silent sergeant on his dais disappeared. Now Benny was alone in a long room with one high window focusing its light upon him. Time passed, a minute or a day. The friendly champion materialized, bringing with him a stranger who laced Benny's arm with tape like a mourning band and began to ask him questions.

'Where were you on the night of . . .'

Benny, frightened now by the machine and feeling too alone, tried to direct his answers to the man. But the man, intent not upon him but upon the machine, registered nothing. Only the machine registered Benny's answers, and only then did the man, watching the machine's strange penmanship, nod and continue. With each line of hieroglyphics that appeared, the friendly detective grew more elated, while Benny, eager to please, saw his answers fall upon deaf ears. He grew jealous of the machine. He hated it.

Then, while the machine finished with him and the man who served it tenderly adjusted its parts to their resting places, the hostile detective, the prosecutor dedicated to his innocence, opened the distant door and walked toward them without, however, seeming to draw near.

Benny's detective, beside himself with joy, called to the newcomer, 'It's the truth. He's telling the truth. He's guilty.'

And the stranger who served the machine looked up and nodded confirmation.

'Well,' said the newcomer, 'he's crazy then. I've been to the hotel where he works. Five people and a bird will swear he was on duty the night of the crime. So he's Superman.' He extended his leg the long length of the narrow hall-like space and prodded Benny's foot with his enormous shoe. 'Get out of here. Get your kicks someplace else, Tony.' Then he turned his back on them. The distant door, too small for a man to pass through, opened and closed again behind him.

Benny's champion, his face obscure, surrounded by the light from the tiny window, turned and said, 'Look ahere, you can't just come in here like this. There's laws. Regulations! You can't just come in here and *get* yourself arrested. You got to *do* something. What's the percentage, anyway? Let's have it. Out with it! You done something. You're a guilty man if ever I saw one.'

But Benny slowly drew himself up and took himself to the door, which moved back and back, eluding him.

'I've got your number,' the detective called, loyal to the last. 'I've got my eye on you. I've got your fingerprints!'

Hands in pockets, Benny Ricco stood before the police station and squinted into the peculiar light, slowly perceiving that it was late afternoon. He meandered to the park and sat on the bench facing the steeple. The squirrels came, and the pigeons, to peck around his feet. He pulled threads from the frayed cuff of his uniform jacket, dropped them on the ground, and waited for the pigeons to steal them. The pigeons ignored his offering. It was not the nesting season. That was past. He considered going to the cemetery to try again to find the grave. But he hadn't energy enough for that. He thought of going to the star-shaped corner to wait for whatever would happen. But instead he sat for a long time, watching the old priest, Father Verciglio, walk up and down, up and down before the rectory, praying his office. Benny was still there when the priest went in.

When it got to be dark, he drew himself up, wondering if his job were waiting for him at the hotel. He decided he would go and see. But he found himself following the walk that led to the center of the park, a place he seldom visited, where among tangled vines and oleander the paths all met, converged upon a statue on a pedestal, a patinaed statue of a man with bird droppings on his shoulders and upturned face. At the foot of the statue he knelt. He tried at first to pray, but the prayers were cotton in his mouth. He tried to recite the catechism, but found he could get no further than chapter one, for kindergartners. Yet it seemed imperative that he speak, and keep on speaking.

He began to say his a-b-c's, got lost several times in the middle, had to begin again, finally arrived at z; he counted to one hundred, said a poem he'd had to memorize in high school, ending, 'I am the captain of my soul,' pledged then allegiance to his flag, and out loud started the multiplication tables. When the street lights came on, Benny Ricco merely closed his eyes and, to the former governor of his state, kept right on praying.

THE QUIET ENEMY

H E HAD never slept with an ugly woman
before, and he was pleased to discover that
how they looked didn't make any difference,
for this discovery solved the only remaining problem
in his life. Since all the women he'd had seemed to get
as much out of it as he did, it had always galled him to
have to shell out money. But it was particularly irri-
tating now, when he was bent upon putting into
perfect practice his much earlier conceived and afterwards mulled over plans for reducing his life to its
simplest denominations. The law of supply and
demand was one he thoroughly understood and
approved. According to it, it was reasonable to suppose that if the woman were ugly enough a man
would not have to pay her, as he'd be doing her a
favor.

It was with similar ingenuity that he had met and
solved the problems incurred by the fulfillment of his
needs for food, shelter, and clothing. He had built his
house with his own hands at a total cost of $483. It was

a one-room concrete block house with three windows, one dead center in each of three sides, and a door dead center in the front. He didn't put in plumbing because that's what runs up costs sky high, and he cooked and heated with a stove he'd bought from a junk dealer for two dollars. He'd only had to go down twenty-three feet to strike water, and his one luxury was a hand pump instead of a bucket. He didn't build a privy because he didn't require one for his simplest needs, and he could always walk up to the filling station on the highway. He solved the problem of food by buying up pigs and calves when they were young, fattening them on the unused portion of his ten acres, butchering and salting them away himself. He bought all of his clothes at the Army Surplus Store where they could be had for less than their original cost to the taxpayer. These problems solved, he could congratulate himself upon having made his way thus far without a by-your-leave from anybody since he'd left the Christian Ladies' Home for the Friendless at the age of fourteen.

He'd left the Home and gone directly into the Marines, being big for his age, and he'd come out of the Marines with eighteen hundred dollars saved. With part of that he'd bought the ten acres of land just outside the only town he could think to return to, the town he'd understood he'd been born in, not forty miles from the Home where he'd grown up. He'd bought the land for a song and started collecting wrecks and selling parts until he had a going concern.

His house was furnished with front seats, back seats, jump seats, an auto radio, auto clock, auto lights, auto mirrors, and he'd rigged his own generator, largely from parts he'd got from his yard, so that he didn't need to pay for city electricity. He slept in a jungle hammock that he'd bought for $6.98 at the Army Surplus and strung from the rafters. He had found that he could make his living out of what other people threw away or sold for next to nothing. This did not injure his pride, for he didn't have any of that kind. Rather, it convinced him that he was smart enough to let other people unwittingly provide for him and make him a self-sufficient man.

Self-sufficient, that is, in all needs but one. Before he'd chanced upon the ugly woman, he'd thought of solving this last of his problems by marrying, though he didn't think he could stand the sight of a woman around his place in the daytime. He hated women as a breed because it seemed to him that a man no sooner got independent of them one way before he found himself dependent on them in another. But he didn't marry one as he reasoned it would be like owning an automobile. He didn't own an automobile because he'd have to pay the upkeep on it even when he wasn't using it. He took the city bus whenever he had to go someplace he couldn't get to on foot.

He was not just an unreasonably stingy man. That wasn't it. But his philosophy of life was a simple one he'd worked out solely from experience. Lacking money puts one in chains, having money sets one free.

It was that simple, and he was certain it was right, the key not to happiness—for he didn't believe in it—but to successful defense against the world. He saw the world as a slaughter block and every man's life as a battle to put off the ultimately inevitable victory of the world and the mass of all other men together. You had to be smart to get by, had to keep your dukes up, and, above all, had to hold on to money—for money, he knew, was the only thing he had to bargain with. He felt that the constant drain made by the simple needs of food, shelter, clothing, and women was the quiet enemy, the deadly enemy, that most let slip up on them from behind and rifle their pockets. He had seen to it that this enemy would not, in his case, find an easy mark.

The most immediate of his needs were solved, then, by early fall of the year he left the Marines. The last solution, involving the ugly woman, was not found until the time when the chill winds of November had settled in, slamming the door to his house, stirring the slivers of ice in his creek, and setting his hammock to a gentle, swaying motion in the night.

Though he'd moved into his house in the summertime when he could bathe in the creek that ran under a bluff at the back of his property, when fall came he began casting around for some less astringent arrangement and happened upon the Bull Chute Truck Stop Café.

The Bull Chute Truck Stop Café was considerably more than just a café. It was built onto the front end of the big auction sheds where cows, bulls, sheep, pigs, goats, and horses from all over the state were put on the auction block every Wednesday from seven in the morning until ten at night. Aside from the café and auction pens, the place was also a filling station that sold not only regular and ethyl gasoline, but diesel fuel as well. Auction pens, café, filling station—and there was also, out back, a bunk house with a shower that made the Bull Chute the most popular truckers' stop for a hundred miles in either direction. You could go by any time, day or night, and find at least three or four big trailers parked out front. According to the sign, the proprietor sold bed and bath for $1.50; bed, bath, and breakfast served at any time of day for $2.00.

He was drawn to the place because he had always heard it said, and did not doubt, that where truckers congregate, there you are likely to find the best and cheapest food in town. He had always had a weakness for dining out, though he did not often these days indulge it because he could cook for himself cheaper. Though throughout the summer he had admired the business sense of the Bull Chute's proprietor, whom he had never met, it was not this admiration, nor even his knowledge that good food was to be had there cheap, that took him up the highway for a visit. It was, instead, his need for a bath.

He walked up the highway early one morning and, from a distance, saw someone putting up storm windows at the front of the café. Before approaching, he read once again the sign that advertised the shower. He had made up his mind what he could offer for a permanent arrangement, but he wanted to get his ceiling price fixed in his mind so he would not impulsively leap above it.

As he approached, the figure manning the screwdriver turned, and he was somewhat surprised to find it was a woman.

'Nice weather,' he said, being pleasant because, though he'd decided on a reasonable price, he intended to drive a better bargain if he could.

She straightened and turned and he saw two shrewd whisky-colored eyes looking out at him over a nose sharp, thin-edged, and slightly hooked so that it looked like a beer-can opener or the beak of some kind of fowl. She was as tall as he was, big in the shoulders and narrow at the hips. Her straight haircut looked like a man's haircut grown out too long. She was so much like a man he thought it unlikely that a man had ever looked at her. And he knew at once that she was the ugliest woman he had ever seen.

After she'd looked at him, she turned her face to the sky and studied the white clouds whisked by the wind at a fast rate overhead. 'Won't be for long,' she said.

'I seen your sign,' he said.

'Which one?'

Now he noticed that the front of the place was decorated with dozens of signs that he had not noticed before since they had nothing to do with him. The one directly over the door they stood under gave the name of the place and, in smaller letters underneath, added, 'Bitsy Finletter, Prop.'

'The sign about the shower,' he said.

'You want a bunk?'

'I live down the road a ways and I got my own bed,' he said as she turned again to her work. 'But I was thinking I might could take my baths up here if the price was right.'

At the mention of price she straightened and turned again, weighing the screwdriver by its handle and pointing its sharp end at him in a way that, under other circumstances, might have been menacing. 'Well,' she said, 'I don't know. I never had a customer just wanted regular baths before.' She narrowed her eyes upon him as though she were determining his relative dinginess so that she might know how much water he would require.

'I don't make much off of baths,' she said. 'They're just what you might call a come-on to help sell bunks and dinners and diesel fuel. I don't know as it would be profitable.'

'I bring my own soap,' he said.

She let the screwdriver slip into the deep leg pocket of her army fatigue coveralls, and leaned on an elbow against the building. 'You don't drive a truck?' she asked.

'No. I don't. I run the parts yard down yonder a ways.'

She nodded. 'Well, you eat though. I reckon we

might work out a plan if you'd care to take a dinner here at the café. On Friday nights the regular seventy-five-cent dinner is fried chicken. I serve it with mashed potatoes, stewed tomatoes, and string beans.'

He calculated in his head. A can of beans was fifteen cents, a can of tomatoes twelve. Without a refrigerator, he had to eat whatever he opened in one meal or let it go to waste. He figured that chicken, tomatoes, potatoes, beans all for seventy-five cents was a bargain it would be foolish to pass up. But he would not agree until he found out what she intended to charge him extra for the bath.

Nodding, he said, 'I reckon if the bath isn't too much extra, we might work us out a deal.'

Now she looked down at the gravel, leaning her head over to her hand in order to scratch and to figure. 'I might could let you have dinner and bath for a dollar fifteen cents,' she said.

'Split with you,' he said. 'Make it a dollar even.'

'Friday night's a busy time,' she said.

'I'd be a steady customer,' he said.

'You say you bring your own soap?'

He nodded.

She straightened, put out her hand, and they shook on it. Then she squatted, balancing on her toes, and went back to work, so there was nothing for him to do but leave. He felt that he'd driven a good bargain. Seven dollars and eighty cents a year for baths, if put against the cost of plumbing, was foolishly cheap. He'd been prepared to go higher.

He planned a schedule whereby he would take his bath at six on Friday evenings, drying and dressing in time for an early dinner at a quarter to seven. To get to the Bull Chute in time, he closed the parts yard at five thirty and put his cash box back in the hole under his floor. Then, on a sudden decision, he opened the box and took out a five-dollar bill and two loose nickels. One dollar was for his bath and dinner, the two nickels were for bus fare to town and back. He had decided that, since once at the café he would already be halfway to the bus-stop corner, he might as well take care of his other need on Fridays as any other night in the week. The remaining four dollars were to pay for that.

The Bull Chute was crowded when, combing his wet hair, he looked in at the door. It was almost seven o'clock. The counter stools were all but one occupied by truckers, and the tables were filled with country families in town for Friday night shopping, when stores stayed open until nine, and dinner out. He sat down at the only remaining counter stool and waited for Bitsy Finletter to take his order. She had a fat colored man for a cook and you could watch him at work through the window between the big aluminum coffee urns. Bitsy took orders and yelled them back to the cook and handed them out when they were ready. She still wore the fatigue coveralls, but now she had on a white apron with a towel pulled through the tie about her waist. To keep her brown hair out of her face, she had stuck two black hairpins, like stunted,

denuded wing-feather ribs, straight back in her hair on
a level with the tops of her red-rimmed ears. When she
wasn't busy taking orders, shouting them to the cook,
handing out coffee, wiping tables, she sat behind the
cash register on a stool and read the evening paper. The
place was quiet but for the sound of frying, of coffee
cups being set in saucers, and occasionally of someone
blowing his coffee cool. So whenever she found something interesting in the paper, she read it out loud.

'Says here,' she said, after she'd taken his order, put
down a glass of water in front of him, and returned to
her seat behind the cash register, 'temperature drop
expected tonight down to thirty degrees lowest this
time of year since 'thirty-two.' And a little later on,
'Pregnant woman shot by spouse baby delivered slug
in hip still alive.'

He enjoyed his dinner, the quiet decorum of the
crowd, the free newscast, the steamed-up interior of
the café, and the condensation on the windows in
which now and then some forward child would trace
a picture.

'Says here,' Bitsy read, 'eight inches of rain below
last year and ten below year-before-last says if we
don't get snow in the winter and a good wet spring
the wheat crop won't make and we'll be in for a
drought.'

When he left the café, it was with a feeling of well-
being. He had to walk another half-mile up the highway to get to the city bus stop, and once on the bus it
took twenty-five minutes to get to where he was

going. Where he was going was to Miss Darlene
Dalrymple's Home-From-Home for Working Girls,
as the square white sign creaking on its hinges under
the orange porch light said. The Home-From-Home
had a large room in the basement with a sign over the
door that read SERVICE MEN WELCOME, and another just
inside that said NO DRINKING OR CURSING ALOUD.
There were chairs against the wall and a small space
for dancing and a pool table set in one end of the room.
There were signs pasted around that read TURN OFF
LIGHTS WHEN NOT IN USE, HELP US KEEP THIS PLACE
CLEAN, BE LADIES AND GENTLEMEN AT ALL TIMES, TOO
MUCH SOAP CLOGS THE MACHINE. And inside the men's
room, built out from one corner, there were two more
signs. One said KEEP FLOOR DRY TO PROTECT SELF AND
FRIENDS, and the other, over the toilet, said WE AIM TO
PLEASE, YOU AIM TOO, PLEASE.

Miss Darlene was a plump blonde woman with
legs like sausage links and hair as fine and dry and
crinkled as cotton. She wore a bright, teary-eyed
smile at all times, and she talked endlessly to whoever would listen about her family in Mississippi. It
had been the ultimate sacrifice, she said, for her to
come even this far north, but she had made it in order
to be with her daughter Dolly Dalrymple, who was
the large, horsy girl that actually ran the place and
kept from her mother the real nature of the business.
Miss Darlene was satisfied that Dolly's friends and
boarders were the nicest group of girls in town, every
one of them ladylike. And she presided over the

basement room in her black lace dress with a bunch of cloth violets at the throat until ten o'clock when her daughter sent her off to bed. After that, the lights went out and the Home-From-Home apparently closed for the night.

When he punched the doorbell, it was eight o'clock. He waited in the hall while Dolly sent a friend up to him. As he waited, he was a little on edge because the week before he had caused a small disturbance when he became convinced that the army was getting first choice in everything. He took the four dollar bills out of his pocket and folded them lengthwise into a hard slat, which he stood slapping against his thigh. When the girl mounted the basement stairs and stood before him in the blue hall light, he knew that he'd never seen her before and that, unlike the other girls, all redheads or blondes, wearing costly layers of make-up, she was ugly. He stood there looking at her, slapping the bills angrily, and let the insult settle to the depths of him.

She smiled, showing a gap between her two front teeth large enough to have accommodated a third, and asked him did he want to see her.

He unfolded the bills, spread them like a hand of poker, took out two, refolded them, and put them back in his pocket. 'I've got two dollars here,' he said, holding up the remaining bills. 'You want them or not?'

She laughed hoarsely. 'Two dollars gets you half-way to where you're going, honey,' she said. 'That's all right with me.'

188

He felt his face burn with a consuming anger. He put the remaining two dollars in his pocket and said, 'If I had a face like yours I'd powder my butt and walk backwards.' And he slammed out onto the porch and stood a moment, shivering, deciding whether or not to go back and hand her the whole four dollars. He took the money out and looked at it, and seeing it there, still in his possession, was what made up his mind. To take himself out of the way of temptation, he hurried back up to the bus stop and had a fifteen-minute wait on the unsheltered corner in the full face of the wind. Overhead, the sky looked like an old woolen army blanket hovering, about to descend. He'd seen dead men covered with them on the frozen ground after an assault, waiting to be taken somewhere and buried, while a tall officer, his face hidden by the shadow of his helmet, moved among them, collecting necklaces until his fist looked like he was carrying a giant ring of keys. He congratulated himself upon still being alive.

On the bus bound again for home, he took out the four bills as a kind of comfort, refolded them into a neat little knot, and punched them deep into the pocket of his pants, where he kept fingering the pill they made until it was slick with sweat.

He got off at the city limits, cold and unsatisfied, and started trudging up the highway toward his turn-off. When he passed the Bull Chute, he decided to go in for a beer, maybe two.

The place was empty except for a driver having a

late supper while Bitsy gassed up his truck out front. Sitting down at the counter, he shoved his hat onto the back of his head and waited for her to come in and take his order. The Negro was gone for the night and she went back to the kitchen herself and got it.

He wiped the bottle top in the hard cup of his palm and had his first drink while the trucker paid silently for his gas and his supper. Bitsy rang it up and the trucker opened the door and left.

The cold draft from the door caught him in the neck and he shivered. Bitsy came to lean across the counter and take up an early edition of the morning paper. He could see she meant to keep him company while he drank, but he didn't listen to the news. As he swigged the beer down few items reached him, for he was thinking in his dull anger that even Bitsy Finletter was not much uglier than the girl they'd tried to foist off on him.

'Tornado toll in millions East St. Louis at mercy of looters bullet baby still alive Christ goes back in Christmas Jesus dolls on sale eight-fifty virgins less do-it-yourself crib kits . . .'

He finished his first beer sullenly and asked for another. Bitsy gave up reading to him and began cleaning behind the counter, wiping the big rough towel over all free surfaces, and now and then looking at him, cat-eyed and curious. He drank silently, tossing the bottle high and slamming it down on the counter to let it rest a minute between his cupped hands.

As he finished his third beer ($ .90) he said, 'You

know there's women in this town can be bought for four dollars? Any woman that can be bought ain't worth the money.' This rationale, only that minute discovered, gave him a pleasant feeling of righteous indignation.

She looked at him and away without answering. She took the left-over slices of pie from under the glass top and put them in the refrigerator.

'Why should I pay them if they don't pay me?' he asked, out loud but speaking more to himself than to her.

Then his eyes focused on her and the idea, the solution, came at him immediately. If he'd taken time to think about it he might not have said anything, but the anger and the beers in him did not allow for hesitation. He said, 'I've got the needs of every other man. And you've got them too. You keep your money and I'll keep mine.' He'd put the empty bottle down and sat staring at the back of her neck.

Bitsy Finletter's first impulse was to turn and knock him flat on his back. But she did not. If anyone had asked her what it was she would least like to be, and she'd answered truthfully, she would not have said deaf, dumb, halt, or blind. She would have said female. It seemed to her that Providence must have sat a long time on her egg pondering what handicap would be the most amusing to give her and had come up with— female! And yet she herself had not been the most disappointed. The most disappointed had been her father, who'd given her the nickname 'Bitsy' (her legal name was Rosy Dawn Finletter, though no one now alive knew it but she) when she shot to within an inch of being six feet tall before she was thirteen years old, and who'd early set out to make a son of her in spite of nature. He'd died, leaving her unfinished at the age of sixteen.

Her first impulse was to knock him flat, and the first reflection that stopped her was the memory of him standing at the cash register earlier in the evening. He was as big as she was. The second reflection that stopped her was that, though knocking him flat might not be a feminine thing to do, the impulse behind it was. She felt she must be as bold, as cool, as to-the-point about it as he, in order to prove herself.

She turned and looked at him and saw a tall, raw-boned, hungry-looking, thin-skinned man, red with cold and angry-eyed. She swiped the towel across the counter in front of him and said, without so much as a blink, 'O.K.' and surprised herself with her own directness. She was heartened by the little glint of surprise she saw in his steel-colored eyes.

He finished his beer, paid for all three, and, after she'd locked the door and put out the light, followed her to the back rooms where she lived.

This was not Bitsy Finletter's first experience. It was her second. The first had occurred when she was eleven years old—the same day she'd tried tobacco. The one experience, she had taken to. She had used tobacco regularly ever since. The other she found distasteful because, like everything else, it favored the male with the upper hand. He was not drunk on three beers, she was sure of that. But he went straight about his business. If he'd tried any foolishness, like kissing her, she would have thrown him to the floor. But he did not. When he angrily mumbled something about being careful, she said don't bother, insulted at the suggestion that she was in some way more vulnerable than he and hence in need of protection. She looked upon what happened as a kind of endurance contest that came out a draw.

After that, he simply came a bit later on Friday nights for his dinner, afterwards taking his bath, and coming from the shower house when the last trucker had pulled out and she was ready to close for the night.

Bitsy Finletter had not expected it to be a continuing thing. She had thought to show him once-for-all and have done with it. On several occasions she thought she would get the place closed before he returned to the café. But she could have the key in the door, ready to be turned, and still he would loom up out of the shadows and push in on her. It's true she could have closed a few minutes early and thereby tricked him. But she would not allow him to interfere in any way, not one whit, with her established pattern of business. She preferred going through with it to that.

They did not for a long time talk on these occasions, each being occupied with some silent challenge to the other. He would come in, sit at the counter, and order a beer. When she brought it, she brought a second bottle for herself even though the taste of beer was not to her liking. After he had finished his, he would slap down thirty cents on the counter, and so as not to confuse her bookkeeping, she would pull out thirty cents of her own and ring up both sales.

If they talked at all, each of them avoided the sense of having started it by leaping to the middle of a subject. He might comment in this way, 'Yep, it's growing all right.' And after a full minute had passed without a question from her, he might elucidate with, 'Growing by leaps and bounds. Yessir, I got all the business I can tend to by myself.'

And if she didn't answer, he would feel his own glibness as a betrayal of some kind of weakness.

Or, if he didn't speak at all, she might say, 'I'm losing money right down the line on it. I ought to raise the price of coffee to a dime.' And as often as not he wouldn't answer either, but would sit looking smug in the knowledge that, this night, he had won out, for she had betrayed the weakness of her feminine nature with careless chatter.

Some nights it was a draw and neither of them spoke at all before retiring to the back room. She would not switch on the lights because there was light enough coming from the liquor store's neon signs across the highway. She would stop on the right of the bed and he would circle to the left by the window. Then, their backs to each other, they would sit on opposite sides of the bed and remove their shoes. To save on laundry, he'd take off his shirt and fold it on top of his shoes on the floor. Then, still without turning to each other, they would lift the edge of the covers and crawl in to lie on the edges of the bed, arms folded beneath their heads. And there'd be another contest, while he waited to see if she wouldn't make the first move. She never did.

Afterwards he would leave quietly by the side door without looking at her or saying good-bye, and she would lie looking at the ceiling until the sound of his footsteps outside on the gravel had died away.

When several months had gone by, he came in tired one night from having set up block and tackle and pulling a motor out of a wrecked Mack truck, and she herself had had a busy day for spring was coming and she'd been waxing floors and cleaning windows and painting outside trim.

She locked the café door after he came in and set two beers on the counter. He took out thirty cents and put it down, and she matched it with three dimes of her own. Then she flipped on the television hanging from the corner of the ceiling and they moved to a table to watch the late show, a Western. By the time it was over they'd had six beers apiece and were feeling sleepy. So, both forgetting to pay the inimical cash register, they moved back to her room, which was large and square with a bright linoleum floor, a clothes press, a straight chair, and a bed. They both went immediately to sleep and they both woke up because of the beer when it was about three A.M.

This was when they had their first conversation.

He said the only time the world was pretty to him was when it was still dark and you couldn't see it. He said he'd spent his life in barracks of one kind or another, first the Home for the Friendless and then the Marines, and he didn't mean to give up his independence now he had it to join with anybody. He said also that women were a weak and shiftless breed and he was glad to be shut of them.

They did not at first talk to each other, but just made comments out loud to the darkness.

He said he went into the Marines because it offered him more money than anything else had at the time.

She thought it was a good reason and she was surprised. Most of the soldiers she'd had occasion to converse with over her counter were young recruits from Fort Leonard Wood who, if they mentioned it at all, talked pompously of saving the world from the Reds or doing their duty. And she'd long felt that all men were sentimental fools. Take Daddy, she had often said to herself, the reason why he wanted me to be a boy was just because he'd been a boy himself when he was young.

Even though she would rather have been a man than a woman, she was a good deal more critical of men than she was of women. She knew this was contradictory and irrational, but that didn't bother her. She knew that the only way to make people seem rational was to lie about why they were the way they were, to squeeze and poke and corset them into some pattern they did not naturally fit.

'The reason why I run this café is because Daddy left it to me. I have improved it in every way better than it was when he ran it,' she said. 'He spent his time going to the auctions on Wednesdays and playing checkers the rest of the week. He didn't have any of what you'd call a business sense.'

'There's not many that has it,' he said.

'My Daddy didn't care if he made a dime so long as he had a cold beer and a checker game going. All he cared about. Start something and let me finish it.'

'You take that Home for the Friendless. I couldn't for a long time make out how come them to run it. They was these well-to-do ladies and they never made a cent off of it that I could see. This young one that taken a shine to me, I ast her oncet how come them to run it and she said because it'd pay their way to salvation. Had all the money they could use so they didn't need to think about anything sensible. I known all along they must of thought they were getting something out of it. Tickled me, because they were going to wake up one fine day and find out they'd th'own away a lot of good money. Salvation's just an idea dreamed up by people that don't know how to get what they want out of the one life they got.'

He said it like he thought he was telling her something. But as it was her time to talk, she wasn't going to waste it by saying he didn't need to tell her for she knew it already. Instead, she steered back to the subject she was more interested in.

'Only thing you can place any faith in's money,' she

said. She said money was the only thing you could count on because it only changed hands, not its nature. She said everything else changed so that you couldn't depend on it. People died, summer went into fall just when you were getting used to it, and they were out to move the highway from her door and ruin her business. She said if she could have chosen what she would be she would have picked a rock, a large rock half buried on a mountainside out of the way someplace.

'I don't depend on people,' he said. 'Listen, you don't have to. You can slip your living in under other people's. I know a man made forty dollars last fall just poking around the dump and picking up electric fans people threw out. Nothing but a rurnt plug or a burnt cord you could fix with a nickel's worth of tape. Known a man oncet sold rocks th'own away out of the lead mines, and he made a living at it.'

'Move that highway a quarter-mile just to straighten out a curve and they straighten me right out of the truckers' trade and my tax money helping them to do it,' she said.

'Known a man oncet had this peculiar stomach he couldn't eat regular food. It would of cost him a fortune just to feed hisself. Listen, they fed him three meals a day and let him sleep in a hospital bed if they could just have his turds for medical science.'

'I always had a good stomach,' she said.

'I rurnt my stomach in the Marines.'

'Where all were you at with the Marines?' she asked.

'I used to could pronounce it,' he said. 'When I came back I bought a map and looked it up. But I couldn't find it because foreign names don't spell out the way they're said. I couldn't say where all I been.'

'Sometimes I wisht I had of been in the war,' she said.

He said it wasn't a thing glorious about it. Just noisy and stinking and a lot of bad food and she ought to be glad she missed it. 'They never told you what it was for,' he said. 'I never known what it was for till I got back and found out about all this prosperity.' He said he had never had the good fortune to be on the end that got something out of things. 'Like the Christian Ladies' Home for the Friendless. The Christian Ladies were who got something out of it, not the Friendless. The Friendless was just what they used,' he said.

She said she'd had a friend once named Maudie Justice, but she died of blood poison at the age of twelve.

And he said the one thing he had that was not on a cash-and-carry basis was insurance against sickness. He said he kept it after he got out of the Marines because doing heavy work you were likely to lose a finger or a toe or a hand, and this insurance paid you good money for it if you did.

'Daddy had burial insurance,' she said. 'But I don't. It stands to reason they won't just leave you lying around and I don't think much about it.'

He said he didn't either, that he must have killed at first hand a dozen times in the war and it didn't make any difference to him one way or another. 'If you're dead, you're dead,' he said. 'No need to make a fuss about it.'

She said it didn't matter to her, for life was not like they said it was.

He said he knew it. He said take songs and picture shows and there wasn't a true thing in them. 'You take all that love,' he said. 'I never in my experience found it to exist.'

'All you can depend on not to die or change is money,' she said.

He said you couldn't entirely depend on that. 'Take you buy a five-pound sack of sugar and pay sixty-three cents for it. But how do you know it didn't cost them just twenty-three cents to put it up?' He said he'd rather pay a hub cap for a sack of sugar. That way he'd know better what he was doing.

She said he was right but there wasn't anything perfect.

Dawn was beginning to mar the eastern sky when he took his leave of her. And he'd walked halfway home before he realized he hadn't got what he went after.

The week that followed was no usual week for him. He found himself doing things he would not ordinarily have done. For one thing, a yellow shepherd dog came out of the woods and tried to take up with him. He chose a half-brick and raised his arm to lam it into the dog and run him off. But when the dog just stood there cowering by the fence, obviously expecting the brick to fly, and yet not running, he lowered his arm, marveling, and though ignoring the dog, allowed it to stay. He didn't at first waste food scraps on it, for he ordinarily buried garbage to enrich a small patch of ground he was preparing for a garden. But one night the dog rewarded him for not throwing the half-brick. A couple of boys tried to steal some tires, and the dog raised such a racket he'd waked up in time to avoid being burglarized. After that, the dog got the scraps. This was unusual.

Another thing he found himself doing was thinking. Usually he was too occupied to think about anything but business. But now he found himself reflecting upon things he'd thought he'd forgotten. This surprised him. But what surprised him more was to discover one night as he lay awake in the comfortable curve and darkness of his jungle hammock that he was thinking in words, as though he were telling somebody his thoughts. It did not occur to him to pay Bitsy Finletter an unscheduled visit. But it was as if what all they'd spoken had cast a spell on him, as if the word had power to stir him deeper than he'd been stirred before. And he was preparing for Friday night. He was collecting carefully—choosing, discarding—those things that he would say. All of them were things he had never before tried to cast into words, but had just let swim around without form or wholeness in his mind. Now he struggled to give form and frame to them so that on Friday he would not make a fool of himself by speaking nonsense.

He had one memory of the time before he was in the Home. It was the memory of a woman in a pink nightgown saying at him, but not *to* him, 'I used to have both health and looks, but now all I've got is him.' She must have said it more than once, because the setting of the memory of it was not always the same. Sometimes it was a room with a cookstove and a bed in it, and sometimes it was outside, on a kind of rotten porch with white things that he thought must have been chickens below in the yard.

He wanted to tell her that. And he wanted to tell her, if he could bring himself to it, about a voice that used to speak in his own head but that seemed to have little to do with him. It said just two words, over and over again when he was in bed at night, until some time when he was around the age of ten it stopped and for a while he missed it and then ever after he had been glad to be shut of it. It whispered, 'I love—I love—I love—'

And there was just one other thought. The head lady of the Christian Ladies, the one they hired to live out there with the Friendless, was a middle-aged woman, still young in appearance and some might have said pretty, for she looked as if she'd never been used for anything. She had a voice that could disguise the meanest things in sweetness, and, because of some terror in her he'd been able to perceive, she planned diligently to deprive the Friendless of any time alone. She had an eye blind to everything but evil. So she sought out evil with a famished curiosity. One morning before daylight he had waked up knowing she was dead, and when he went back to sleep it was with a kind of peace he had not known before. He'd waked again at six to find the place in a quiet frenzy. He'd known before they told him what it was about. And always afterwards he'd taken credit to himself for killing her, as if by willing it he had seen to its happening. He was looking forward to Friday night with Bitsy Finletter for he was almost sure he could tell her these things and, by telling them out loud, be rid of them forever.

These things—the dog and the thoughts—were unusual. Another unusual thing was his belated discovery that Bitsy Finletter was not ugly. This he could not understand. He had never questioned that she was the ugliest woman he had seen. But he no longer saw her that way. It's true he didn't see her as pretty either, but the way he saw her neither prettiness nor ugliness entered into it. He felt he had discovered something that, though not negotiable, nevertheless had value to it, a value for him alone. It belonged to him as did his own big toe, and cut off from him would have no worth whatsoever. So he felt secure in the possession of it, did not have to worry about losing it or setting a price on it. This same thing had happened to him once before, when he was small and worried about not owning anything, even the pants he wore. He'd discovered one night, by thinking, that he owned himself, that if anybody tried to use him in any way he could become stiff as a board, deaf, dumb, and blind if need be, and keep himself inviolate. The ladies had a large garden patch that they used the Friendless to cultivate. He had found that he need not work in it. He could resist by lying still in bed, not listening when they threatened, not focusing his eyes on them when they hovered over him. And there was nothing they could do about it. He'd eventually gone back, of his own accord, to hoeing the patch, but it was because he got some pleasure out of it, not because they could make him do it. It had been the most remarkable of his experiences to that time. Afterwards he always knew he belonged to himself and nobody could use him. Now he knew that his particular vision of Bitsy Finletter belonged to him also and that no one else could have it.

And the last of the extraordinary things that happened to him came when the week was almost up. What happened was: the voice came back to him. He awoke one morning feeling himself not alone, and found it had come back to him some time in the night. It followed him about in the daytime as he stacked tires, cleaned old parts with gasoline, dried out carburetors in the sun. It followed him about whispering its two words as if it were trying to tell him a secret but hadn't adequate enough vocabulary at its disposal. It followed him about, whispering down from somewhere above and behind him, as though it belonged to someone much taller than he was. And it said as it used to say when he was a child, 'I love— I love—I love—' It was like the words to a song he didn't remember hearing but couldn't get out of his head. That had happened to him before and was the only experience he could connect this one with. 'I love —I love—I love—' it said. And he found he was not displeased to have it back.

On Thursday night he did not sleep at all and hardly closed his eyes. Friday morning a customer was successful haggling him down on a set of white-wall tires. Friday noon he opened a can of sardines for his lunch and sat on his stoop feeding every last one of them to the yellow dog, who quivered all over with pleasure. Friday afternoon he cut his hair with much taking of pains, using two auto mirrors, one before and one behind. At five o'clock he closed the yard even though a hot-rodder thundered up and wanted in to look for a certain type of timing gear which he knew he had and could get a good price for. He closed even though he intended to keep to his discipline and stay away until his usual time. Then he meant to walk to the café, eat, take his shower, and go to her at nine o'clock. For some reason it seemed very important to keep to his rigid Friday schedule. He did not want to be late, however. At nine o'clock he wanted to begin talking right away because he wasn't sure he could get said all of what he wanted to say before next daylight came.

Bitsy Finletter, on the other hand, was not looking forward to seeing him, had, in fact, no intention of seeing him ever again. Her week, too, had been unusual, for during it she had made a discovery that, though she could not easily believe, she could nevertheless not deny. Though ugly, she was a young and healthy woman, regular in all things, and her time of the month had come and gone and she had for three mornings running been deathly ill and tossed up her breakfast before nine o'clock. Not only that, but she also could not stand the taste of tobacco, and, like a drinker tapering off, she had developed a craving for sweets, which she had never liked before, her natural preference running to fried foods, hot bread and butter, and heavily salted meat.

Now, though she sat at the cash register each night, she no longer read the news aloud or even to herself. She sat despondently, eating candy bars off the counter in front of her and ringing up at regular intervals her nickel sales to herself. She felt her size for the first time as a handicap, for what she would have liked to become was invisible. She neither blamed nor hated him. Nor did she blame or hate herself. What she blamed and hated was something she had always felt was not a regular part of her, though attached like a growth or tumor. She blamed her femaleness. And now she saw what she felt she had known always but had not understood till now—she saw that this femaleness had been the destruction she had carried in herself from time before she was born and that the simplest acts of eating, sleeping, and avoiding being run down on the highway had nourished and kept it as they nourished and kept the healthy part of her. She had been doomed by Providence sitting on her egg, and she now suspected that she was not alone, but that the meanest man, woman, and child alive also carried some joke of Providence in his unsuspecting person, be that joke no more than death itself.

It's true she thought of forcing him to marry her. But she saw at once that would be a womanish punishment for them both, and beneath her. She had not had time or presence of mind to work out the details of a plan of action, but she knew some broad objectives that grew out of her nature and took no thinking about at all. She knew that no one must see her in such a condition, not because of any shame growing out of a sense of immorality or sin found in public places, but because of a private sense of shame growing from this proof of her sex. She knew she would find a place where she could wait and then be delivered in perfect privacy, and she pictured this place as a kind of desert, barren of all growing things, where not even animals would choose to live. She would deliver it herself and then she would give it to the first person she met and be rid of it. After that, she would be herself once more.

As for seeing him again, she had no intention of it. She felt that in some uncanny way he would know at once when he set his eyes upon her. And she did not mean to give him that satisfaction. The challenges were over, and she meant for him to think they had come out a draw, a deadlock.

She meant to stop serving dinners at seven thirty

that night, to close and lock the door just before eight. It did not occur to her that he might come early, because that breach would prove a weakness in him and give a small triumph to her.

She closed at five to eight, letting the cook go without washing up the remaining dishes, and locked not only the front door, but the door to her room as well.

At eight o'clock she heard his footsteps crunch gravel out front, heard him pause a moment—he must have been amazed at the dark café—heard him try the door, then rattle it a little. For a while, then, she didn't hear anything. And she knew he'd gone around the other side to have his shower and, perhaps, to puzzle over this strange turn of events. She enjoyed for a moment the mystery she had created, the puzzlement she'd given him.

She waited, sitting fully dressed on the side of her bed, for twenty minutes. She wanted to be sure he had gone before she went to bed. She hoped to hear his footsteps cross in front of the gasoline pumps and then to see him in the light of passing cars as he walked back down the road and away.

At ten minutes to nine she decided that he had gone the other way, toward the city bus stop, that he was at this moment halfway across town, and she nodded to herself, glad to have it over. At nine minutes to nine, when she'd risen and begun to undress, she glanced at the window and saw his silhouette outlined by the liquor store's light. She stood perfectly still in the partial dark, her fingers on the top button of her coveralls, close to her heart so that she felt the startled fury of its beating.

For a moment he did not say anything. He seemed to be listening, trying to hear if she were there. She breathed shallowly.

But when he spoke, his voice told her he had divined her presence in the room. He'd spread one hand and put it on the screen, and the shadow of the hand reached gigantically in to hold her against the far wall. 'Why'd you lock me out?' he asked.

She didn't answer.

'Let me in. I've got to talk some more,' he said, and listened again a moment to hear if she would speak.

'Let me come in. Listen, what I want is to talk some more. I won't lay a hand on you if that's what's bothering you. I want to talk. I swear. I want to talk and that's all I want.'

She said, 'Talk where you are. You're talking all right.'

And then for a time he was silent.

'You're doing all right,' she said. 'Go on ahead and talk. Say what you want to say and then get on off. I don't plan to have any more to do with you.'

The hand moved away from the screen and down to his side. The shadow of it gone, she was sure he could see something of her there against the white wall.

'Say what it is you come to say and then get on off before I call the law,' she said.

'Listen, I want to say some things,' he whispered.

But the light wind dispersed his whisper so that only the sibilance of it reached her. Sure now that he could see her anyway, she moved across to sit on the edge of the bed next to the window, for she was curious about the strangeness of his request, his voice, the docility with which he stood pleading.

She wondered if she would let him in after all. She told herself he could not yet know what her weakness had done to her, and that was, after all, the reason she had not wanted him to see her. She knew she could not have stood the humiliation of his knowing, for it proved them unequal that she should be caught while he went free.

'Please open the door and let me come in,' he said. 'I've got a need in me—a big need in me to talk. I got some things in me need to be said out loud and not sieved through any screen. Let me talk. Oncet. Let me talk and then I'll get on off and won't come back again.'

She didn't answer, for she was occupied with trying to see his face, if it matched the strangeness of his voice, see what this change was that had taken hold of him. She began to feel the stir of some secret pleasure she could not yet name, some pleasure that diminished or covered up her own shame until for a moment she was not aware of it. But she could not clearly see his face, only the tip of his nose that was illumined in the slanting, colored light.

She got up, went to the door, and slid back the latch. He sprang across the space from the window and pushed the door with an urgent shove. It banged against the chain lock she had not loosed. A little laughter bubbled inside her, but did not break out.

'Wait a minute,' she said. 'Not so fast.' And she pushed the door closed so she could take off the chain. Then she went back to sit on the edge of the bed, and he followed to sit beside her, his big hands between his knees, pressed together.

Now she could see his face in the dim light, could see little spots reflected in his hidden eyes, the lax hang of jaw, the solemnity of his gaunt cheek.

'What is it?' she asked.

His mouth worked silently once, and then he began, hurriedly, to speak, as if he recited some poem or address he'd memorized. His voice was a monotone and his speech so fast that she could not make out much of what he said except for a word or phrase now and then. In the midst of his talk, his teeth would suddenly chatter and a rigor catch him up. As it was not that cold, she thought he might be drunk, and she leaned close to him to see if she could smell whisky on his breath.

When she leaned to get a whiff of him, he reached quickly and took hold of her shoulders. He stopped speaking for a moment, and when he spoke again she clearly understood what it was he was saying. She had not heard this voice before. It was as if a voice not his own spoke out of him to say, over and over again, 'I love—I love—'

Startled, she looked at him, suspecting either that

he'd gone suddenly mad or that he had in some uncanny way found out and was making fun of her. But
in the blinking light she could see the deep holes his
eyes made in his bony face. And she could see that
this face was filled with a bleak and helpless terror
such as the terror she had known all through the week.
She saw, furthermore, that in some way less tangible
than her own, he too had been caught. The knowledge filled her with relief at first, and then she felt the
little hint of pleasure return, more powerful this time.
It seemed to give her back herself and her strength.
For she understood that he had been caught in a way
she had not been caught, that she would again next
year be whole and that he might never be.

She did not often laugh out loud, for she had early
found that the things that made her laugh did not
make others laugh, and laughing alone calls attention
to oneself. But now she was laughing before she knew
it. And then, after one startled moment when he
seemed to come to himself, he hit her, hit her across
the mouth and she tasted the salt taste of blood. She
did not lift a hand to defend herself, but laughed out
again at the knowledge of her triumph. Each time the
pain of his blows shot through her, she laughed again.
This knowledge of victory gave her the pleasure he'd
not given her before, and she could not stop laughing.

He thrust her off the bed onto the floor and once
more she laughed. And that's when she felt his boot
hard in her stomach.

She did not hear him leave, but when she came to

her senses he was no longer there. She pulled herself up and into bed, and she did not for a week rise out of it. The cook left food outside the door for her at night, and she crawled to get it like some scavenging animal. For a time she thought she would die. But on the third day she was relieved to know it was only the thing that had been alive inside her that had died.

'I'm shut of it,' she said out loud to herself. 'I'm free.'

After that, her strength came back to her, and she knew that the real part of her had retreated to some place deep inside her where it would evermore be safe.

At the end of the week, when she found she could stand up, she dressed, climbed into her jeep, and drove to the parts yard, knowing already what she would find but having to see for herself.

She pulled up in the road out front, yanked her hand brake, and sat with the motor running. The gate was closed with a chain and padlock, but a group of small boys had climbed the fence and were exploring among the wrecks. The empty one-room house was wide open, with a starving yellow mongrel sitting in the door. A hand-painted for-sale sign, already riddled with bullet holes, had been knocked askew on the fence.

As she sat there, eying desolation, she thought of him off someplace in his barracks bed again. She felt close to him in a kind of conspiracy, certain that she had given him his freedom in return for her own, and that they were now even.

And finally as she sat there, gunning the motor but not yet driving off, she was overcome with a great and weighty sense of pity that made itself felt in the chords of her throat. She was sure it was not pity for herself or for him. She was sure the pity was for the mourning mongrel yellow dog, deserted, perhaps to starve, the one victim she could think of left in the wake of the wind that bore their troubles away.